**"Thank you. I'm going to be
stuck here a long time without your
help. Know of any motels nearby?"
He pressed his lips together with a
frown, and looked down the road.**

"We don't have any motels in Tipton." Lauren
debated her next words, and prayed she
wasn't making a mistake. How could she drive
away and leave him behind? "My aunt and I
live just a few miles away. You could stay in
our guest room if you like."

His brown eyes studied her for a moment.
"Okay. Thanks, I'd appreciate that."

She held out her glove-covered hand. "My
name's Lauren Woodman."

He shook it with a firm grasp and smiled.
"Wesley Evans."

Warmth and gratitude traveled through
her. Though he'd initially made her wary,
something made her trust him.

And yet, questions rose in her mind. Why was
he hiking alone down this road? And what
brought him to Wild River?

CARRIE TURANSKY

Carrie Turansky and her husband, Scott, live in beautiful central New Jersey. They are blessed with five great kids, a lovely daughter-in-law and an adorable grandson. Carrie homeschools her two youngest children, teaches women's Bible studies and enjoys reading, gardening and walking around the lake near their home. After her family lived in Kenya as missionaries for a year, Carrie missed Africa so much she decided to write a novel set there to relive her experiences. That novel sits on a shelf and will probably never be published, but it stirred her desire to tell stories that touch hearts with God's love. *Along Came Love* is Carrie's debut novel with Steeple Hill. She loves hearing from her readers. You may e-mail her at carrie@turansky.com. You're also invited to visit her Web site at www.carrieturansky.com.

ALONG CAME LOVE

CARRIE TURANSKY

Steeple
Hill®

Published by Steeple Hill Books™

STEEPLE HILL BOOKS

Steeple
Hill®

ISBN 0-373-87363-8

ALONG CAME LOVE

Copyright © 2006 by Carrie Turansky

www.SteepleHill.com

Printed in U.S.A.

For as high as the heavens are above the earth, so great is His love for those who fear Him; as far as the east is from the west, so far has He removed our transgressions from us.

—*Psalms* 103:11–12

This book is dedicated to
John and Shirley Turansky, my husband's parents,
who have loved me like one of their own.
For fifty years they have walked together on a
path of faith and love that will bless generations
to come. I thank God for them, and I treasure the
love and laughter we have shared.
Happy anniversary, Mom and Dad!

Chapter One

Heavy snowflakes flew toward Lauren Woodman in a swirling cloud. Gripping the steering wheel, she leaned forward, straining to see through the snow-spattered windshield. The approaching dusk and dancing flakes limited her view to no more than a few yards ahead. She slowed and shifted to a lower gear. At this rate, it would take her at least fifteen minutes to drive the last few miles home.

She sighed, knowing it would be better to arrive late than end up in a ditch or stuck in one of those waist-high drifts lining the road.

A movement up ahead caught her attention. She squinted as though that would clear her frosty windshield better than her groaning wipers. A man was hiking along the roadside, his head bent into the wind and driving flakes.

What on earth is he doing so far out in the country on a night like this?

As she drew closer, the beam of her headlights illuminated him. Tall and broad-shouldered, he straightened and turned toward her car. The steel-framed backpack he was carrying accounted for some of his bulk but not all. He wore a dark knit hat pulled down to his eyes, and some sort of snow-caked scarf covered the lower half of his face. He lifted a gloved hand in the universal sign of a hitch-hiker.

Lauren's heart thudded. She couldn't stop. He was not only a stranger but most likely homeless or deranged, to be out in this weather.

Help him find his way home, Lord. She fixed her eyes on the road ahead and drove past. As soon as she got back to her aunt's house she'd call the police. They'd pick him up and help him find shelter until the storm passed.

She lifted her gaze to the rearview mirror and he came into view. Resigned to being left behind, he hunkered down into the wind and trudged on.

Suddenly, a flash of brown darted across the road in front of her car. Lauren gasped, jammed her foot on the brake and jerked the steering wheel to the left. Her car skidded and spun like a sickening carnival ride.

A scream tore from her throat. Clutching the steering wheel, she frantically pulled it to the right. The snowbank loomed before her. She made one last desperate attempt to swerve away, then rammed into it with a crashing thud.

A deathly silence roared in her ears. Her heart pounded in her throat, choking off her air. Pain ricocheted through her shoulder and neck, where the seat belt held her in place. Through her daze she heard rapid footsteps crunch across the snow, and then someone rapped on her window.

"Miss, are you all right?"

The sight of the stranger peering through the side window jarred her back to her senses. He opened the door and the interior light flashed on.

Lauren stiffened and pulled back. He wasn't wearing a scarf. A dark, shaggy beard and a frozen, snow-covered mustache hid the lower half of his face, giving him a wild appearance.

"It's okay." He leaned in and gently laid a large glove-covered hand on her shoulder. "Are you hurt?"

Frosty, pine-scented air flooded the car. She pulled in a sharp, cold breath and her thoughts cleared. "Yes, I…I'm fine. But what about my car?"

With trembling hands, she pushed her long red hair over her shoulder and reached to unhook her seat belt. A frustrated moan escaped as she struggled with the latch.

"Maybe you should just sit tight and rest a minute more. I'll check it out for you."

She looked up at him and was surprised by the gentle concern in his dark eyes.

"I'm okay, it's just this crazy seat belt," she insisted, finally releasing the latch.

He stepped back and plodded through the snow toward the front of her car. "I don't think you've done too much damage," he called over his shoulder. "Good thing you missed the deer. That could've totaled your car."

His deep voice cut through the snowy evening silence and sent a shiver down her back. She slowly leaned out the open door, watching him.

Who *was* this man—a threat or a rescuer?

With a sinking feeling in her stomach, she realized it was too late to slam the car door and lock herself inside. She was stuck in the snowbank and needed the help of this rough-looking stranger if she was going to get out.

Oh, Lord. Should I trust him?

Summoning up her courage, she climbed from the car to check the damage herself. Teeth chattering, she fought to control her wobbly legs and settle her runaway emotions.

"How are you doing?" He turned toward her.

"I'm all right." She reached down and brushed away a layer of snow. "Oh, no, look at it!" The impact had crumpled the fender and smashed it into the tire.

Spending the barn renovation money on a tow truck or car repairs would force her to push back the opening of her gallery, but if she filed a claim, her insurance would skyrocket. "I really don't need this," she whispered past the tightness clogging her throat as tears stung her eyes. *Stop! It won't do any good to cry, especially in front of a stranger.*

He squatted down to take a closer look at the damage. "Don't worry. I can get you out of here." He scanned the woods beyond the road, dropped his pack from his shoulders and climbed over the snowbank.

"What are you looking for?" she called, standing

on tiptoe to watch him. The storm had slowed and the late-afternoon sunlight reflecting off the snow made it a bit easier to see.

"Here's what we need." He pulled a sturdy limb from a downed tree that lay just a few feet from the roadway. Hoisting the limb over his shoulder, he hauled it back toward her and climbed over the snowbank to the road.

"What are you going to do with that?"

"Ever take physics?" He shrugged the limb off his shoulder and dropped it to the ground near the front fender.

"No, why?"

"Physics teaches you how to think scientifically." He grinned, his dark eyes glowing with humor. Suddenly he didn't look nearly as frightening as she'd first imagined. Certainly, his beard looked unruly, but his coat and boots looked clean and well cared for. Perhaps he wasn't a homeless wanderer as she'd first suspected.

"Are you a physics teacher?"

"No, but it was one of my favorite classes."

"Not me. I avoided science whenever possible."

He lifted his dark brows and smiled. "Well, it's never too late to learn the principles of physics." He wedged the limb between the tire and the crumpled fender. "This is a first-class lever." With a swift thrust, he forced his end of the limb toward the ground. The branch groaned, the fender screeched and what she could see of his face flushed with the effort.

Lauren stood back in surprised silence as he

lifted the crumpled fender away from the tire. When he finished, he heaved the limb over the snowbank and sent it flying into the woods as though it weighed no more than a broomstick.

"Let's clear away some of the snow from the front tires," he said, brushing off his gloves. "Then we'll try to start it up and back it out."

Lauren pointed to the trunk. "I've got a shovel."

"Smart lady," he said with a little chuckle.

His comment warmed her all the way down to her boots. It had been a long time since she'd received any words of affirmation from a man. She popped the trunk, retrieved the collapsible shovel and carried it up front.

"Here, I'll take that." He stepped forward and held out his hand.

She hesitated a moment, gripping the handle. He could obviously do the job quicker, but she didn't like to depend on anyone else. Well, this was no time to hang on to her pride. She passed him the shovel. He quickly cleared the front of the car while she brushed off the hood and windshield.

"Okay. Why don't you see if you can start it up?"

She climbed into the driver's seat. Whispering a prayer, she turned the key. The engine coughed and sputtered but soon smoothed out to a consistent purr. She slowly eased the car back a few feet.

He grinned and gave her the thumbs-up sign.

She set the emergency brake and hopped out. "Thanks. I might've been stuck here a long time without your help."

"No problem. Glad you're okay." He turned and

walked toward his heavy pack lying in the snow-
drift.

Fiddling with her wet gloves, she watched him.
How could she drive away and leave him behind?
It wouldn't be right. "Where are you headed?"

He hoisted the pack onto his shoulders. "Wild
River Ski Resort." Instead of asking if she was going
that way, he quietly adjusted the straps on his pack.

Frightening memories swirled to the surface and
Lauren forced down a shudder. "That's a long
way—at least seven or eight miles."

Frowning, he pressed his lips together and looked
down the road. "Know of any motels nearby?" He
turned to her with a hopeful lift of his brow.

"We don't have any hotels in Tipton." She bit her
lip, debated her next words and prayed she wasn't
making a mistake. "My aunt and I live just a few
miles down the road." She gave a little shrug. "We
have a guest room. You could stay with us if you
like."

His dark brown eyes studied her for a moment.
"Okay. Thanks, I'd appreciate that."

Lauren held out her glove-covered hand. "My
name's Lauren Woodman."

He shook it with a firm grasp and smiled.
"Wesley Evans."

Warmth and gratitude traveled through her.
Though he'd initially made her wary, something
told her to trust him.

"You can put your backpack in the trunk. There
should be plenty of room. Just shove those paint
cans aside."

She slid into the driver's seat and glanced at him again in the rearview mirror. Had she made the right decision, inviting him home? Wesley slammed the trunk and pulled his knitted hat down to his dark eyebrows. As she forced her gaze away from the mirror, questions rose in her mind. Why was he hiking alone down this road? And what brought him to Wild River?

Chapter Two

Wes felt like a fool, sitting in the passenger seat dripping all over Lauren's car as the snow melted off his hat and ran down into his beard. Her windows were getting steamy, and with each passing mile his defrosting coat smelled a little more like an old wet sheep. He stifled a groan. She must think he was really strange.

"Are you from around here?" she asked, sending him a quick sideways glance.

"Nope." Uneasiness tightened his chest. He turned and stared out the side window, praying she wouldn't ask any more questions like that. The less anyone knew about him the better. He still couldn't get used to tiptoeing around the truth, but he didn't want to talk about where he'd spent the past two years. It would only stir up more questions—questions with painful answers he didn't want to share with anyone right now.

His gaze drifted back toward her and he pondered the strange set of circumstances that had brought them together. Earlier, he'd prayed someone would stop and give him a ride—he just hadn't expected it to be someone young and pretty like Lauren.

Watching her car skid off the road had sent his adrenaline pumping, and when she'd climbed out of the car, shaking and tearful, the urge to reach out and comfort her had been difficult to fight. Instead, he'd focused on fixing her car, hoping that would ease her worries and get her back on the road. But somehow he felt he should do more to help her.

"This is Long Meadow." Lauren pointed to a large two-story farmhouse painted soft butter-yellow set back from the road in a field of sparkling snow. Several windows on the first floor glowed with golden light. She turned in and drove down a long driveway between two rows of large maple trees, their branches laden with snow.

When they pulled in and parked at the side of the house, he spotted a few shutters that needed to be replaced and some sagging gutters, but Long Meadow was a beautiful historic home with unique character. The house seemed to say, "Welcome, come in and stay awhile, make yourself at home."

He blew out a slow, shaky breath and looked away. The invitation wasn't for him. He'd only be in Tipton long enough to figure out what to do next. He doubted he'd ever be free to settle down in a place like this.

He hesitated as Lauren flipped on the car's interior light, unfastened her seat belt and reached for her purse.

At this close range, he could see the fine dusting of cinnamon-tinted freckles covering her creamy skin and the fullness of her coral lips. She brushed a lock of wavy red hair away from her cheek, sending a whiff of soft, flowery fragrance his way. The scent stirred some distant memory.

Wes swallowed and closed his eyes, blocking out her image. He wasn't free to entertain the idea of getting involved with Lauren Woodman or any woman. Not now. Maybe never. There was too much pain in his past. Too many unknowns in his future. Though it wasn't intentional, he always seemed to hurt the people he cared for most.

Moments later, Wes stomped his boots on the mat outside Lauren's back door. Had he made a mistake accepting her offer to stay at Long Meadow? She didn't seem to recognize him. Maybe she didn't follow the international news. More than five months had passed since his release from prison in the Middle East. Hopefully, that was long enough.

The wet snow fell from his boots in slushy clumps. With a frustrated glance, he realized he would probably track quite a bit in with him. Lauren pulled open the back door and stepped through ahead of him. The smell of savory beef and fresh-baked bread wafted out, making his mouth water and his empty stomach rumble.

"You can hang your things here." Lauren pointed to a row of wooden pegs along the wall of the combination mudroom and laundry room. She slipped out of her hunter-green wool jacket and green plaid scarf and hung them next to a child's yellow rain slicker. She tossed her brown leather gloves into a wicker basket at their feet. They landed on top of a few other pairs of brightly colored mittens and gloves.

Wes leaned his pack against the wall in the corner, then shrugged out of his heavy coat and pulled off his hat and gloves.

"Is that you, Lauren?" A sweet, older voice called from the steamy kitchen just beyond the mudroom doorway.

"Yes, it's me." Lauren glanced at him with a hint of uneasiness in her eyes. Did she regret her invitation now that she was safely home?

"I brought someone with me," Lauren called. "Can you set an extra place for dinner?"

As he followed Lauren into the kitchen, he ducked his head to miss the top of the doorjamb. He probably wouldn't have hit it, but it seemed close enough to make him wary.

An elderly woman wearing a brightly flowered apron looked up from stirring something in a saucepan on the stove. Her friendly expression and twinkling blue eyes looked a lot like Lauren's.

She wiped her hands on her apron. "Well, hello there. Welcome to Long Meadow." She extended her hand, not seeming the least bit bothered by his wet, rumpled appearance. "I'm Matilda Woodman, but please call me Tilley." Her face and hands were wrinkled with age, but her warm smile and gracious manner made the wrinkles fade from view.

"This is Wesley Evans. He's on his way to Wild River and got caught in this storm."

"It's nice to meet you, Mr. Evans. Dinner's almost ready. Would you like to wash up first?"

"Yes, thanks," he said, surprised by the easy way she welcomed a stranger into her home.

Walking with a slow, stiff gait, Tilley showed him to a small bathroom just off the kitchen. He thanked her and closed the bathroom door. Looking in the mirror, his startled reflection stared back at him. Flecks of melting snow still glistened in his bushy beard, and his overgrown, dark brown hair stuck out in all directions, except where his hat had smashed it down on top of his head.

He scowled at his reflection. This untamed look helped disguise his appearance, but he definitely needed a haircut and shave soon. Tonight he'd just wash up and run a comb through his hair. He wasn't trying to impress anyone. It didn't matter what they thought of him.

He grabbed a small black comb from his back pocket and held it under the water as guilt washed over him. He ought to care. How could he share the Good News if his wild appearance made people think he was a scruffy wanderer? He turned off the water and tapped the comb on the side of the sink.

Well, that wasn't his concern anymore. He planned to get a regular job and stop worrying about the spiritual needs of everyone he met.

But how could he ignore the tug of the Holy Spirit? Could meeting Lauren simply be a coincidence with no divine plan behind it?

Chapter Three

"Where's Toby?" Lauren asked as she set a steaming platter of meat loaf and potatoes on the kitchen table.

"I sent him up to change out of his wet clothes. He'll be down in a minute." Tilley's old blue eyes sparkled with interest. "Where did you meet Mr. Evans?"

"He stopped to help me on Johnson Creek Road. I had a little trouble avoiding a deer."

An anxious frown settled over Tilley's face. "I hope you didn't damage your car."

"It'll need a little work, but it's not bad." Lauren prayed she wasn't stretching the truth too much, but she didn't want her aunt to worry.

"That was certainly nice of him to stop. I'm afraid most people would've just driven right on by."

"He wasn't actually driving." Lauren placed a

folded napkin next to the extra place setting. "He was hiking."

Tilley's silver brows lifted. "I can't imagine anyone hiking in this weather."

Uneasiness rippled through Lauren. Why had Wesley Evans chosen to hike to Wild River rather than drive? If he was too poor to own a car, how could he afford to stay at a ski resort?

"Who's goin' hiking?" Lauren's six-year-old son, Toby, trooped into the kitchen with Tilley's black-and-white Border collie at his heels.

"No one is going anywhere tonight," Tilley said. "There'll be another foot of snow by morning."

"Hey, sweetie." Lauren reached for her son and scooped him up for a tight hug. He giggled as she tickled him in the ribs and placed a sloppy kiss on his neck. Bryn barked happily while Toby wriggled free.

"Did you wash your hands yet?" Lauren asked.

"Yep." He held them out for her to inspect and sent her a broad grin, displaying the gap where he'd lost his two front teeth. His toothless smile flew straight to her heart and she could barely resist grabbing him again for another delicious hug. Instead, she nodded her approval and ruffled his blond hair.

Lauren had many regrets about her past. Being a single mother had never been easy, but Toby brought more joy into her life than any other relationship she'd ever known. She never thought of him as a burden, but as evidence of God's grace in her life—well worth all the sleepless nights and endless worry that came with parenthood.

The bathroom door opened. She looked up as Wesley walked back into the kitchen. His time in the bathroom had done little to change his untamed appearance.

Bryn rushed forward, barking. Toby stiffened and his mouth dropped open as he stared up at Wesley.

Lauren reached for the dog's collar. "Down, girl. It's all right." She waited for the dog to relax and then placed a reassuring hand on her son's shoulder. "Toby, this is Mr. Evans. He's having dinner with us and staying overnight as our guest."

Her son sent her an apprehensive glance.

"Hi, Toby." Wesley lifted his hand and smiled.

Toby melted back against Lauren's leg, though he watched the man with wide-eyed interest.

Wesley didn't seem bothered by Toby's response. He squatted in front of Tilley's dog and held out his hand. The dog hesitantly sniffed his fingers. A moment later, her tail waved like a flag in the wind as she licked his hand.

Wesley smiled at Toby. "You've got a nice dog. What's her name?"

"Bryn, but she's not mine. She's Aunt Tilley's." Toby stroked the dog's back. Then he looked up and flashed Wesley a shy smile.

Lauren's heart warmed. Toby's hand looked so small compared to Wesley's, but they both stroked the dog with the same gentle touch.

"Bryn's a good dog," Tilley added. "She's been my companion since my husband George passed away." She untied her apron and hung it on a hook by the refrigerator, all the while watching Toby and Wesley pet Bryn. "Now both you boys need to wash your hands again. Go on. You can use the kitchen sink." She waved them away.

Lauren stifled a chuckle as Wesley followed Toby to the sink. Toby pulled up the small wooden step stool and Wesley turned on the water. She smiled as she watched them work together under the watchful eye of her aunt.

"That's better." Tilley handed them a towel. "Now let's sit down before our dinner gets cold." Tilley smiled at their guest. "Mr. Evans, why don't you sit right here between Lauren and Toby."

Warmth crept up Lauren's neck as she sat down next to Wesley. Lauren knew her aunt meant well, but romance was the last thing on her mind. Overseeing the renovations that would soon turn their barn into Long Meadow Art and Antique Gallery and helping her son adjust to a new school and home were more than enough to keep her busy. Besides, her past gave her little confidence where men were concerned.

Toby climbed into his chair and held out his hand to Wesley.

"It's our habit to say grace before meals." Tilley looked at Wesley. "Perhaps you'd like to lead us?"

Lauren blinked. Why would Tilley put their guest on the spot like that? She opened her mouth, intending to offer to pray, but Wesley reached for her hand and sent her a calm, steady look that stilled her words. He bowed his head. She held her breath and closed her eyes.

"Father, thank You for the warmth of this home and the kindness of this family. It's good to sit in a circle and remember You and Your love."

Wesley's deep voice vibrated through Lauren and sent shivers racing along her arms. The startling difference between Tilley's cool, frail hand and Wesley's warm, expansive grasp made it hard for her to focus on his words.

"We praise You for Your goodness toward us," Wesley continued. "We thank You for Your constant care and especially for Your hand of protection over Lauren tonight. We're grateful for this food that's been so lovingly prepared. Be with us now as we share this meal and send down Your blessing on this home and all who sit around this table tonight. In Jesus' name, amen."

Lauren swallowed and quickly blinked away a tear. How could such a simple prayer touch a place so deep in her heart?

As soon as he lifted his head, Wes reached for his water glass and took a long drink. He hoped his prayer hadn't sounded contrived. He was a little rusty, but he meant every word he'd said. He still struggled to understand the difficult path the Lord had taken him down over the past two years. But that didn't mean he'd lost his faith. He'd simply decided he needed to change his vocation.

"Thank you, Mr. Evans. That was lovely." Tilley beamed.

He relaxed and returned her smile. "All my friends call me Wes."

"All right, Wes, why don't you tell us about yourself? Any man who prays like that must have a story to tell."

Wes coughed and took a second drink. "There's really not much to tell."

Tilley chuckled. "Now don't be modest. You're among friends. Tell us where you're from." She placed a small serving of meat loaf and a few potatoes and carrots on her plate then passed the platter to Lauren.

He let out a slow, deep breath. "I grew up in Portland, Oregon."

"Well, that's certainly a long way from here. What brings you to Vermont?"

Wes accepted the platter from Lauren with a small nod. What would they think if he told them how far from Oregon he had traveled over the past few years? He immediately decided against it.

"I'm interviewing for a job at Wild River Ski Resort. I have a good friend who works there." Everything grew quiet. Wes glanced around the table.

The color seemed to drain from Lauren's face. "Who's your friend?"

"Bill Morgan. He's the head naturalist at the Nature Center. Do you know him?"

Lauren nodded and seemed to relax. "Yes, he attends Tipton Community Church with us." But the unsettled look in her eyes sent a wave of apprehension through Wes.

Bill had assured him his past would not be an issue in this small community, but how could he avoid the questions that would undoubtedly arise? He wouldn't lie. His faith and his conscience wouldn't allow it. But he would have to be more careful, especially around inquisitive people like Tilley and Lauren.

"So you're moving here to Tipton?" Tilley asked as she buttered her roll.

"Yes, ma'am. If the job at Wild River works out."

"I want you to call me Tilley. That's what all my friends call me." She chuckled and continued. "Tipton is a wonderful little community. A fine place to settle down and raise a family. That's why Lauren moved back here."

Lauren quickly glanced at Tilley.

"And I couldn't be happier about that," Tilley continued. "I was so worried about her when she lived in Boston. That's no place for a single mother to raise a son. Coming home to Vermont has been a wonderful arrangement for all of us. But that isn't the only reason she—"

Lauren cut her off. "I'm sure Mr. Evans isn't interested in my reasons for coming back to Tipton."

"Nonsense! Of course he's interested."

Lauren's painful expression breached the protective wall Wes had constructed to keep everyone at a distance. Heaviness flooded him, almost as if the burden she carried had been transferred to his shoulders. He pulled in a deep breath, uncertain if he wanted to listen to the Holy Spirit's promptings. But the impression would not leave.

"I'd like to hear what brought you back to Tipton."

She wiped a smear of ketchup off Toby's chin and then looked down at her plate. "Maybe some other time," she murmured.

Who was responsible for the sorrow he saw etched on her face? Then an even more disturbing question penetrated his thoughts. What was he going to do about it?

Chapter Four

Lauren padded into the kitchen, longing for a cup of coffee and one of Tilley's apple-walnut muffins. She'd smelled the tantalizing aromas all the way upstairs.

"Morning, Tilley." She crossed the kitchen, took out a mug and pulled a spoon from the drawer.

"Good morning." Tilley wore a red-checkered apron tied over a black sweater and pants with a red turtleneck peeking out underneath. "How did you sleep, dear?"

"Not too well." Lauren yawned, recalling her restless night. Each time she'd closed her eyes, the alarming image of her car spinning out of control and smashing into the snowbank replayed through her mind and every frightening sensation flooded her again. Then dreams featuring their guest disturbed her sleep until well past midnight.

Lauren couldn't imagine why she'd dreamed

about Wes. He didn't seem to be a threat, though he'd told them little about himself. He prayed like a man who knew God in a personal way, and he'd totally captured Toby's heart. Perhaps that was what made her uncomfortable.

Last night after dinner they'd spent a quiet evening playing board games with Toby and her aunt. Wes had tended the fire and taught Toby how to roast a marshmallow to golden perfection. She smiled, recalling her son's sticky grin.

So why should Wes flood her dreams and make her uneasy?

Lauren took a sip of coffee and felt its comforting warmth flow through her. It didn't matter. He'd be leaving as soon as they plowed the road. "Have you seen Toby yet?"

"He's with Wes, shoveling a path to the woodpile."

"Outside?" Frowning, Lauren set her mug on the table and headed for the back door.

"Don't worry, dear. I made him put on his hat and gloves. They've been at it for about fifteen minutes. I imagine they're about to the woodpile by now."

The sound of a shovel scraping against the cement walk reached Lauren's ears and then the gentle laughter of her son. She pushed aside the sheer white curtain covering the back-door window. Rubbing her fingers on the steamy glass, she cleared a small circle and peeked outside.

Deep snow covered everything except the shoveled pathway. You could now walk from the back door to the garden shed, where the woodpile stood neatly stacked against the south wall.

The new layer of snow had added another foot, bringing the total to well over eighteen inches. Lauren spotted Toby chasing Bryn along the freshly cleared path. Delight filled her son's face as he danced in circles with their aunt's playful dog. Toby's warm breath puffed out in small clouds each time he exhaled. Bryn barked and gallivanted along with him, obviously happy for the freedom of the brisk morning.

Wes stopped and leaned on the handle of the snow shovel, watching her son's antics. His bushy beard almost hid his smile, but his eyes lit up with warmth and laughter. Toby tossed a snowball his way. It missed and fell short, splattering on the walk. Wes reached down, quickly formed his own snowball and returned fire.

Toby ducked and squealed. Bryn leaped in the air, trying to intercept the frozen missiles flying along the path.

Lauren smiled at the scene. Toby needed the company and friendship of a man. She worried about the fact that he had no male relatives nearby. Was that the root of his struggles at school? Perhaps even a brief friendship with someone like Wes Evans would give Toby a glimpse of a male role model and help boost his confidence.

But what if it made his lack of a father more painfully obvious?

Lauren opened the back door and shook off that troublesome thought. She did the best she could on her own. She'd learned the futility of hoping any man would stick around long enough to make a difference—for either of them.

"Time to come in, Toby," she called. "Breakfast is just about ready."

Her son scampered toward the porch, grinning at her with laughing eyes and bright red cheeks. "Me an' Wes shoveled the whole walk!"

"Yes, I see. It looks great. Thanks very much." She kissed his cheek and sent him in to shed his winter gear.

Lauren's gaze drifted past the porch and settled on Wes as he strode back toward the shed, snow shovel in hand. He deposited it inside and shut the door. Then he walked back to the woodpile and filled his arms with a large stack of firewood.

"You don't have to shovel and tote wood. You're our guest," she called, feeling both flustered and pleased. "We haven't even given you breakfast yet."

He smiled. "It's not a problem. I don't mind helping."

She felt herself blush and groaned inwardly. In spite of his bushy beard and rustic appearance, there was something awfully appealing about Wes Evans. It was more than just the usual male-female attraction, she reasoned. His helpful attitude, his kindness toward Toby and his prayer over last night's dinner all spoke to her heart.

"Thanks for shoveling. Now we can get to the cars."

Wes glanced toward the drive. "I don't think you're going anywhere today. The snow looks pretty deep."

"I suppose you're right. We'll have to wait for the county snowplow to come through. Then our neighbor will bring over his truck and plow the drive for us."

"Guess I won't make it to Wild River today."

"I'm sorry you're stuck here." She offered him an apologetic smile.

"Don't be sorry. I'm not."

Lauren blinked. "You're not?"

"No." He chuckled and stepped past her into the house. "Breakfast smells great!"

Wes pushed back from the table with a satisfied sigh and smiled across the table at Tilley and Lauren. "That's the best breakfast I've had in a very long time."

Lauren quickly glanced away, looking embarrassed, but Tilley seemed pleased by his compliment.

"I'm glad you enjoyed it. My husband used to say, 'A hearty breakfast is the best way to start the day.'"

"He sounds like a wise man," Wes added.

"Oh, he was." Tilley's dreamy gaze drifted to the window. After a moment she rose from her chair and began clearing the table.

Wes stood and reached for the plate of muffins just as Lauren grabbed the other side.

"I'll take that." She looked at him with a touch of pride and challenge in her eyes. Yesterday, he would've said her eyes were blue, but today he saw that they had flecks of green and gray. Either way, they were very pretty.

He smiled and gave up the muffin plate, but he took his own dishes and glass over to the sink.

Toby slid off his chair and called Bryn. "Can I give her this?" The boy held up a small piece of muffin.

Lauren turned to her son. "You know the vet says no table scraps."

"But she wants it. Look, she's hungry." Toby gazed up at his mother with a pleading expression that matched the look in the dog's eyes.

A smile twitched at the corners of Lauren's mouth. "No muffin, but you can give her a doggy treat after you clear your place. Even though school is canceled today, you still need to make your bed and do your chores."

"Do I have to make my bed?"

"Yes, and pick up your pajamas, too. Go on. I'll be up to check in a few minutes."

Toby carefully carried his plate to the counter. Lauren passed her son a small bone-shaped dog treat and gave him a playful pat on the seat of his pants.

Toby scurried off toward the stairs, grinning at Wes as he passed. Bryn trotted at his heels, her tongue lolling and her toenails clicking on the hardwood floor.

Wes returned to the table and picked up the pitcher of juice and the little crystal dish of raspberry preserves.

"Oh, Wes, you don't have to do that. Lauren and I can take care of it. Perhaps you'd like to use the phone to call Bill Morgan. I imagine he's at home today rather than at the Nature Center." She pulled open a drawer and began to hunt through it. "I have his number in our church directory."

"Thanks, Tilley," Wes said. "I've got his number."

She chuckled. "Of course you do. You're old friends."

Wes nodded as he thought of his former college roommate. Bill had been a faithful financial supporter and prayer partner for seven years while Wes served as a missionary in the Middle East. Bill's invitation to stay with him in Vermont had come just at the right time. Wes had finished his session at La Ruche, a small center in Switzerland that specialized in debriefing people who had been in crisis situations, and he had been uncertain what to do next.

His sister, Jennifer, urged him to return to Oregon and stay with her. But they weren't close, and Wes didn't feel ready to answer her questions. His coworkers at World Outreach had encouraged him to remain in Switzerland and wait for reassignment. He wasn't comfortable with that option, either. His faith had been deeply shaken. How could he lead others to trust God when his doubts had cost him and those he cared about so much?

So he'd backpacked through Europe for three months and slowly made his way to London. Bill's promise to help him find a job had finally brought him home to the U.S.

"You can use the phone in the living room," Lauren offered, interrupting his thoughts.

She walked out of the kitchen and he followed her, noting the hypnotic way her long red hair swished back and forth in time with her steps. She was a very attractive woman, though she didn't seem to be overly focused on her appearance. He liked the way she dressed in comfortable clothes but had her own unique style that reflected her artistic nature and love of color and texture. He'd discovered her interest in art and antiques last night while they played a game of Scrabble. She'd told him about her plans to open an art and antique gallery when she finished renovating their barn.

All that intrigued him, but her love for her aunt and son impressed him more.

So where was Toby's father? Why would any man walk away from a beautiful wife and a son like Toby? Could Lauren be a widow? He quickly dismissed that idea. Tilley said she was a single mother. That usually meant divorced or never married. Neither seemed to fit Lauren.

Toby thundered down the steps and zipped through the living room. "Bryn needs another treat," he called as he disappeared into the kitchen.

Lauren's perplexed gaze followed Toby. She turned and pointed to the phone on the end table. "Here you go."

"Thanks." He pulled out his wallet.

"I'm not sure how soon they'll clear the road. Sometimes it takes a day or two for them to get out here when it's this deep." The apologetic look in her eyes made him smile. She was either very caring or still a little nervous about him staying another day.

"It's okay." He sorted through the papers in his wallet and found Bill's number written on the back of a London Tube schedule.

Lauren bit her lip, watching him. "I hope this won't ruin your chances of getting that job."

"I told Bill I'd arrive sometime this week. There's no specific appointment yet."

She released a soft sigh. "Good. I know how hard it can be to get a job, even when you have contacts."

He searched her face, pondering her comment. What had life been like for her as a single mother living in Boston, trying to make ends meet and care for her son on her own? Probably challenging and difficult. Yet she was concerned about him finding a job. That touched him.

"Mom!" Toby burst into the living room. "There's water all over the kitchen floor!"

Lauren spun to face him. "What?"

"It's like a big flood!" Toby's eyes bulged with the news.

Lauren gasped and ran toward the kitchen.

Wes pocketed his wallet and hustled after her.

Chapter Five

The sharp edge of the cabinet floor pressed into Wes's shoulders as he lay on his back under Lauren's kitchen sink. He scooted in another inch to see if he could get a better view of the broken pipe. The open drain filled the air with a damp, pungent smell. It made Wes wish he had a third hand to hold his nose, but it didn't seem to bother Toby. He slithered in next to Wes like a little snake.

"How's it look?" Lauren asked as she squatted down to peer under the sink. A worried frown creased her forehead.

He shot off a quick prayer that his knowledge of plumbing would be sufficient to help her. "Could you pass me that large wrench?"

"Sure." She handed him the tool and leaned closer. "Do you think you can fix it?"

"Looks like these two pipes came apart." He enlarged the adjustable wrench and lined up the pipes, hoping he could reattach them. With a grunt and a twist of his wrist, he swiveled the wrench, but the pipes wouldn't hold. Toby scooted closer, watching every move, his breath smelling like the bubble gum he chewed.

"Looks like you'll need a new piece of pipe to fix this. But we can probably hold it together with some duct tape till then. Can you pass me a strip?"

"I'll get it." Toby wriggled back and grabbed the piece of tape Lauren held out. The little guy sure was cute. He really wanted to help. He scooted in again and, as he leaned over Wes, his gum dropped out of his mouth.

Wes felt it land in his hair just above his left ear.

Lauren sucked in a quick breath. "Toby!"

"Sorry." Toby shrank back, looking at Wes with large, fearful eyes.

"Don't worry about it. I'll get it out when we're done. Pass me that tape."

Toby slowly handed him the silver strip. Wes took the little boy's hand and guided it toward the broken pipe. "Would you help me hold this up?"

Toby nodded and grinned, looking relieved. Wes wrapped the duct tape tightly around the pipes and then added a second strip to make sure they would stay put until he could install the new pipe. He grabbed the wrench and slid out from under the sink. Toby scooted out with him.

"Good thing Tilley went upstairs to lie down." Lauren shook her head, still looking a little bewildered. She gathered the wet towels and took them to the laundry room.

Wes collected the tools and set them on the counter next to the refrigerator.

Lauren walked back into the kitchen, her gaze focused on the spot above his left ear. "I'm sorry about the gum."

Wes reached up and found the sticky wad still tangled in his hair.

"Here, let me help." Lauren crossed the room and peered at the gum. "You better sit down. This might take me a minute."

Wes pulled out a chair and took a seat at the kitchen table. Lauren moved closer and carefully ran her hand through his hair, tucking a piece behind his ear. It had been a long time since anyone had touched him so gently. He settled back and released a slow breath, trying not to let Lauren's touch shake him.

During his eighteen months in prison, they'd kept him in a cell by himself with only occasional trips out for brutal interrogation sessions with the prison officials. Though it had been almost five months since his release, those haunting memories sent a sickening wave of anxiety through him. He closed his eyes and breathed deeply, practicing the relaxation techniques they'd taught him at La Ruche to deal with flashbacks. Within seconds the memories faded and lost their hold.

"Toby, how many pieces of gum were you chewing?" Lauren asked.

"Only two."

Wes opened his eyes. The boy leaned on Wes's knees, watching his mom.

"I hope I'm not pulling too hard. This is really stuck."

"No, it's fine." Wes certainly didn't mind. Lauren smelled like cinnamon, reminding him of the muffins they'd all shared at breakfast. He shifted his focus to Toby and studied the little boy's features. He had blue eyes like his mother, but his blond hair and medium skin tone must have come from his father. There wasn't a freckle on his face, while Lauren's heart-shaped face was generously sprinkled with them.

"I got gum in my hair once," Toby said. "Mom had to cut it out."

"Is that right?"

"Yep. But it's okay. She cuts my hair all the time."

Wes glanced up at Lauren. "You cut hair?"

"Well, I cut Toby's." A small smile played at the corners of her mouth.

"Maybe that's the best way to get rid of this gum."

Her blue eyes widened, and she looked at him cautiously.

"I was hoping to get a haircut before my interview."

"Are you serious?"

"Sure, why not? I think that would be a fair exchange for fixing your broken pipe."

She narrowed her eyes. "What you gave me was a temporary repair. Are you saying you'll finish that plumbing job if I cut your hair?"

"Hmm." He scratched his cheek, enjoying the moment.

"Okay. You've got a deal." He'd already planned

to fix her pipes, but he wasn't going to tell her that now. He needed a haircut, and he couldn't think of a prettier barber.

"I hope you'll like the way I cut it."

"Toby's haircut looks good. What do I have to lose?"

She laughed and her blue eyes danced. "A lot of hair!"

Lauren retrieved her scissors, pinned a large towel around Wes's neck and dampened his hair with a spray bottle.

Toby's hyper wiggling made it hard for Lauren to focus, so she sent him to get his headset, a kids' praise CD and a bucket of LEGO blocks. He was now happily building spaceships at the kitchen table and humming along with the music.

Shifting her gaze back to Wes, she ran the comb through his hair and tried to ignore the way he watched her. Warmth rose up her neck and flooded her face. She knew red blotches must be covering her neck and chest by now. Her tendency to blush was bad enough, but those awful blotches announced her runaway emotions to anyone watching. Thankfully, she wore a soft-green turtleneck sweater that hid them from Wes's view.

Why was she feeling so flustered? She'd given haircuts to several male friends in college. Perhaps her reaction had something to do with the fact that she hadn't been this close to a man in a very long time.

"So where'd you learn to fix plumbing?" She

steadied her hands and focused on the comb and scissors.

"My grandpa could fix anything. I spent a lot of time following him around when I was younger."

"So he taught you about plumbing?"

Wes nodded.

"Hey, don't do that or I might cut off a piece of your ear by accident," she teased.

He froze, staring straight ahead. "Yes, ma'am."

She grinned at the funny expression on his face. She liked his warmth and sense of humor. They made her feel comfortable to share a little more about herself. "You were lucky to know your grandparents. I never knew mine. Tilley and George raised me after my mother died."

"What about your father?"

"He sent me to live here at Long Meadow. Tilley is his older sister. She and my dad grew up here."

"How old were you?"

"Just three. I don't even remember my life before that."

"Is your dad still alive?"

"No. He passed away last summer while he was on a trip to Europe with his third wife." She couldn't keep the bitter tone out of her voice.

"I'm sorry."

"It's okay. I hardly knew him." She looked at Wes. What did he think of a father who abandoned his daughter to relatives and had never cared enough to build a relationship with her? She didn't think much of him, and she'd grown tired of making excuses for his behavior. Her kindhearted aunt was more forgiving. Tilley said perhaps he stayed away because she reminded him too much of her mother, Janelle. She wasn't convinced. Thoughts of her father always left her feeling hollow and disappointed. The only good thing he had ever done for her was make her the beneficiary of one of his life insurance policies. Those funds were now paying for the barn renovations and starting inventory for the gallery.

"So you grew up here in Tipton?"

"Yes. I've lived here all my life, except when I went to college in Middlebury and the six years I spent in Boston."

"What took you there?"

The scissors stilled in Lauren's hand. Her mind spun, searching for an honest answer that wouldn't reveal too much. She wasn't about to tell him she'd left Tipton to keep her pregnancy a secret from Toby's father and everyone else. That was a painful story she rarely shared with anyone. After Toby's birth, she'd told her aunt about her son, but she'd stayed away from Tipton. And though people liked to speculate about Toby's father, she'd never revealed his identity to anyone, not even Tilley.

"I guess I wanted to see what life was like away from Vermont." She reached for the spray bottle and squirted the back of Wes's hair again. "Enjoy the glamour of the big city, that kind of thing." She tried to keep her tone light, but she wasn't too successful. Her years in Boston had been far from glamorous. Lonely and disappointing would be a better description. No white knight had appeared to rescue her and her son, and she'd finally realized that facing curious questions back home in Tipton would be better than life alone in the city.

"How did you like Boston?"

"It's a beautiful city, but my fine-arts degree didn't open up too many career opportunities." She moved around to his left side and continued cutting.

"So what did you do?"

"I lived with friends from college and had a number of jobs that didn't go anywhere. After my third roommate got married and moved out, I decided to come back home to Long Meadow. It was time. Toby was ready to start first grade."

"How does he like his new school?"

She glanced at Toby. He looked lost in his own world with his earphones still in place. "Not too well. I'm not sure if it's the move or adjusting to a new situation or something more. He really struggles with reading." As she thought of her last conversation with her son's first-grade teacher, a wave of frustration washed over her. The teacher made it clear she attributed Toby's problems at school to the fact that he had no father involved in his life. Lauren didn't see how that could make it more difficult for Toby to learn to read, but it didn't relieve her guilt.

Lauren sighed and clipped another strand of Wes's hair. "I don't understand why he's having so much trouble learning to read. I've done everything I can think of. We visit the library, I limit TV, we read aloud and I don't even have a computer to distract him." She stopped and shook her head. "I help him with his homework every night, but it just doesn't seem to click."

"He's only six, right? Give him time. He'll catch on."

"I hope so, but his teacher is convinced it's a learning disability or an emotional problem." She hated to admit those two awful possibilities, but sharing them with Wes made her feel a little better. "I'm not sure what to do." She trimmed around Wes's left ear, careful not to nip him with the scissors. "He gets nervous and upset every morning. I can hardly get him out the door and on the school bus. If something doesn't change, he's going to end up hating school." She stopped and clicked her tongue. "I'm sorry. I shouldn't be going on about this. It's not your problem."

"It's all right. I don't mind listening."

She smiled, certain she heard genuine empathy in his voice. "Thanks. Most people act like they're listening, but they're really just waiting until you're done so they can dump a load of unwanted advice."

He chuckled. "Sounds like you need some new friends."

She whisked a few stray hairs from his shoulder. "Not everyone's like that." She thought of Julia and smiled, then combed out the next section of his hair. "So…now it's your turn. I promise I'll be quiet and listen. No advice unless you ask for it."

He shifted his focus to the floor and frowned.

"What? Your life's perfect?" She hoped her teasing tone would bring him back into the conversation.

He lifted his gaze to meet hers. "No, not by a long shot." Reaching out from under the towel, he flicked a piece of hair off his pant leg. "I guess I'd say I'm at a crossroad. I need to make some decisions about my life." His serious tone added weight to his words.

"I thought you wanted to work at Wild River."

"I do, but that may only be temporary."

Slipping her finger under his chin, she raised it slightly to check if his haircut was even on both sides. He looked at her with a painful openness, as though he wished he could say more.

"What did you do before you came here?" Immediately, she felt him tense and his face clouded with uneasiness. She dropped her hand.

"I've done several different things," he said slowly.

Curiosity rippled through her. "Like what?"

He shifted in his chair. "I was a teacher, and I've been the administrator of a small medical clinic."

She smiled, relieved that his previous employment seemed so normal. "Those sound like interesting jobs. Pretty different, though."

He glanced at her again and seemed to relax. "They had some surprising similarities."

Lauren combed through his hair one last time, pondering his comment, but he didn't offer an explanation. She stepped back. "You're all finished. Want to take a look?" Lauren passed him a hand mirror.

He smiled. "Wow, it looks good. Thanks."

"You're welcome." She thought it made a big improvement in his appearance, and if he trimmed his beard, he'd look even better. "What job are you hoping for at Wild River?" She unpinned the towel from his neck.

"I hope I can work with Bill at the Nature Center. He said that would involve teaching groups of children and adults, maintaining the exhibits and leading outings. But I'm open to doing just about anything. I don't even care if it's maintenance. I just need a job and a place to stay so I have some time to…" His words faded off and he glanced back at her with an embarrassed expression.

"Time to do what?" she asked softly.

An unmistakable sadness clouded his eyes. "Never mind. It's not important."

"I'll get a broom and sweep this up. Be right back." She hurried from the kitchen.

Lauren pulled open the closet door, pondering Wes. He appeared to be unusually kind and sensitive, but he was also secretive. His elusive answers made her suspect he carried a lot of pain from his past…and that made her even more curious.

She silently chided herself. A man who wasn't open couldn't be trusted. It was a good thing he hadn't told her any more about himself. She didn't want to know because knowing might mean understanding and caring, and that would be too dangerous for her heart.

Chapter Six

Wes ran his hand over his clean-shaven face and studied the man in the bathroom mirror. New, deeper lines ran from the sides of his nose to the corners of his mouth. People called them laugh lines, but Wes knew they hadn't come from laughing.

He turned his head slightly and stepped closer to the mirror, examining the jagged scar still visible on his left cheekbone. He should've had stitches for that cut, but his interrogators had taken delight in the fact that he carried a visible reminder of their power over him.

Wes pushed aside that disturbing memory and shifted his focus to the new haircut Lauren had given him the day before. She'd parted it on the right and left the top longer than usual, but he liked it. He almost looked like his old self. A wave of uneasiness traveled through him. Was five months long enough for people to forget the media photos they'd seen of him?

Following his release, coworkers had sent him magazine and newspaper clippings they'd saved. Many featured photos of a gaunt man, forty pounds lighter, wearing a haggard expression the day he'd been escorted away from prison in the company of the Swiss embassy official. His stay at La Ruche and travels through Europe had given him time to regain some of the weight he'd lost. Thankfully, he didn't look too much like that half-starved prisoner in the photos anymore.

But would Lauren and her aunt connect his name to those news stories and realize his true identity? He hoped not. He was tired of traveling. Freedom had felt good for a while, but it hadn't brought the peace he longed for. The same difficult questions that filled his mind on the day of his release continued to trouble him no matter where he traveled.

He believed he'd been called to work in the Middle East. So why hadn't God protected him from arrest and imprisonment? Why had he been kept in prison for almost eighteen months when others had been released? Why had he signed that confession and endangered his coworkers and Middle Eastern friends? His lack of faith and courage had hurt those he loved and worked with. He still didn't know the fate of some of his friends.

Wes closed his eyes and took a deep breath. He had to stop torturing himself and put those questions out of his mind. Nothing could change the past. He had to let it go. Take hold of today. That was the only way he could keep those painful memories from holding him captive any longer. At least that's what they'd told him at La Ruche.

But somehow, it was not that easy.

Tossing his bath towel over the rack, he checked the mirror once more. Satisfied, he stuffed his shaving gear back in the small, black leather bag and left the bathroom.

The delicious smell of bacon and eggs floated up to meet him as he descended the stairs. He heard Toby and Lauren in the living room and waited on the landing for a moment, listening to Toby struggle through a reading lesson.

"B…aaa…duh. Ssss…aaa…duh."

Did the boy realize if he connected the syllables they'd actually become words? He slipped into the living room unnoticed and stood beside an overstuffed chair near the stone fireplace. Lauren and Toby sat together on the couch, focusing on the blue paperback book she held in her lap between them. The bright morning sunlight shone through the front window and made Lauren's long red hair glow like burnished copper. Wes smiled. Lauren's love for her family was obvious and endearing, and she had enough spunk and creativity to open her own business. On top of that, she'd welcomed him into her home like an old family friend without knowing who he was or where he'd come from.

"P…aaa…duh." Toby wiggled and rubbed his nose on his sleeve.

"Good! That's it. Keep going." Lauren leaned

forward, her lips silently forming each syllable as Toby labored over the words.

"Mmm…aaa…duh." Toby scrunched his shoulders and released a frustrated huff. "What's that word?"

"It's *mad*. See…" She ran her finger under the letters, slowly sounding them out for her son. "Try the next one."

Toby bit his lip and scratched his cheek. He looked up, spotted Wes and smiled. "Hi, Wes."

"Morning." He returned Toby's smile and stole a quick glance at Lauren.

Her mouth dropped open as she looked at him.

Wes rubbed his bare chin and chuckled. "Do I look that bad without my beard?" He sincerely hoped it was the shave and not some distant memory from the evening news that put the startled look on her face.

Lauren's mouth snapped closed and her face flushed. "No, no, of course not. You look fine. Very…neat." She slapped the book shut and sprang from the couch.

He grinned, feeling tickled that he'd surprised her by his changed appearance. "I fixed that wobbly towel rack in the bathroom, and if you have a Phillips screwdriver, I can take care of that loose hinge on the lower cabinet door."

"You fixed the towel rack?" She blinked her blue eyes.

"Yep." He pulled his Swiss Army knife from his front jeans pocket and smiled. "I've got a flat-head screwdriver right here, but my Phillips was a little too small for the other job."

"Wow, is that a real knife? Can I see it?"

"Sure."

Toby hurried over, his gaze fastened on the knife. Wes squatted down to eye level with the boy and held the knife out for him to examine.

"That's cool! Where'd you get it?"

"I bought it in Switzerland." He didn't think Toby knew where that was, but Lauren's surprised expression gave him a moment's concern. It couldn't be helped. He'd been determined to always tell the truth, even when he was in prison. He wasn't sure if it had hurt or helped his case there, but at least he had a clear conscience in that regard.

Tilley walked in from the kitchen, wiping her hands on a kitchen towel. "Good morning, Wes." As he stood and tucked the knife back in his pocket, she looked him over. "My, don't you look handsome." Her old blue eyes twinkled and she smiled. "Doesn't he look good, Lauren?"

Lauren flashed a glance at her aunt and then shifted her gaze to Wes. "Yes. Very nice." She laid the reading book on the coffee table. "Toby, would you go feed Bryn?"

"Okay. Come on, Bryn."

The dog jumped up from the fireplace hearth and trotted after Toby. The boy took only a few steps, then stopped and ran toward the front window. "Look, here comes the snowplow."

Wes heard the roar and scrape of the plow and glanced outside. The bright yellow truck with a large blade attached in front flew down the road, clearing a path and shoving huge mounds of snow to the side.

Toby groaned. "Does that mean I have to go to school?" He turned pleading eyes on his mother.

She joined him at the window and lovingly brushed the hair back from his forehead. "No, the radio said school is canceled. I guess not all the roads are clear yet."

"Yippee! No school!" Toby danced across the room. Bryn barked and followed him toward the kitchen.

Tilley chuckled and glanced over her shoulder at them. "Breakfast is ready. I just need to pour the juice."

"Okay. We'll be right in." Lauren looked at him with a hint of sadness in her eyes. "It looks like I'll be able to drive you to Wild River today. I expect our neighbor will plow the driveway as soon as he finishes his."

Wes nodded and an odd mixture of relief and regret hit him. He needed to check on the job at Wild River, and seeing Bill would be great. But when would he see Lauren and Toby again? That question bothered him more than he'd expected. A painful hollow feeling hit his stomach, and he knew it wasn't caused by his hunger for breakfast.

Lauren watched Wes stow his backpack in the trunk and they both climbed into her car. Lauren's heartbeat cranked up a notch as she glanced across at him. With his new haircut and clean-shaven face, he certainly looked handsome. It irked her that she noticed it now just as he was leaving.

"I talked to Tilley, but she wouldn't let me pay

anything for staying with you." Wes pulled off his gloves and reached for his seat belt. "I wish you'd let me give you something."

They'd warmed up the car, and it felt wonderfully toasty. Lauren tossed her hat and mittens in the back seat. "No, Tilley and I talked it over." She checked her mirror and turned the car around. "Besides, look at all the things you fixed for us. I'd say it was a fair exchange."

"I wish you'd reconsider."

She smiled and shook her head. "Do you know how much it costs to have a plumber come out in a snowstorm?"

Wes chuckled. "All right. Thanks. I appreciate it."

"You're welcome." Lauren slowed as the road narrowed and they crossed a small bridge. "Seems like something always needs to be repaired in an old place like Long Meadow. I've learned how to paint and refinish furniture, but plumbing and electricity are out of my league."

"I do want to fix that broken pipe for you. When can you get that piece?"

She smiled, pleased he remembered his promise. "I called Les Morris at the hardware store in town. He says he has just what we need. I thought I'd pick it up today after I drop you off."

"Good." Wes nodded. "Then I'll come back to Long Meadow and take care of it as soon as I'm done with my interview." He turned to her, a question in his eyes. "If you don't mind coming back and waiting around for me."

The thought of spending time at Wild River made

her stomach twist into a tight knot. She hadn't been there for seven years, but that wasn't long enough to erase the awful memories connected with the resort.

He studied her face. "It's okay if you have other plans. I'm sure I can hang out with Bill or find something else to do."

She shot a brief glance at him. "No, it's fine. I'll pick up that pipe and wait for you in the lodge."

"Are you sure?" Unspoken questions seemed to hang behind his words.

"Yes." She looked straight ahead, gripping the steering wheel, but her heart and mind screamed, *No!* She couldn't calmly walk through Wild River as though nothing had happened there. Her foolish choices and the harrowing events that followed had changed her life forever.

Lauren silently shook herself. She was being ridiculous. There was nothing to be afraid of now. The man who had stolen so much from her had died in a skiing accident almost a year ago. The news had stunned her, but it had also allowed her to return to Vermont.

She lifted her chin, her determination returning. She would go to Wild River and face her fear. Maybe that would loosen the hold those terrible memories had on her heart.

Wes clasped his hands in front of him and leaned forward. He glanced at his watch and then down the hall toward the lobby of the ski lodge. He'd been sitting on this bench outside Mr. Zeller's office for ten minutes, waiting for his interview—long enough to be tempted by the smell of coffee and hot chocolate drifting toward him from the lodge café.

The voices of skiers and snowboarders returning for lunch made him long for the opportunity to join them. It had been several years since he'd snapped on a pair of downhill skis. There hadn't been much opportunity for the sport while he'd lived in the Middle East.

The office door burst open. Wes looked up and saw the white-knuckled hand of a man grip the doorjamb. The rest of his body remained hidden in the office.

"Just because you're my father doesn't mean you can run my life!" The young man's voice vibrated with emotion. "I'm twenty-seven years old. I deserve a little respect."

"Come back in here and shut the door." The deep, gravelly voice came from farther inside the office.

"No! You're going to hear me out for once." The young man's hand disappeared, but his voice rang through the hallway. "I left a good job in New York to come back here and work with you. But you're driving me crazy. Things have to change or I won't stay."

"Don't threaten me," the older man growled.

"I'm not threatening you. I'm trying to make you understand. I need the freedom to do things my own way without you hanging over my shoulder all the time. I don't want to be treated like a kid."

"Then stop acting like one."

"Come on, Dad!"

"No, you listen to me, Ryan. I've had enough of your wild shenanigans. You'll inherit all of this someday. It's time for you to settle down, face up to your responsibilities and learn how to run this resort."

"I'm not Stephen. I never will be. I need to find my own way." Ryan stormed out the door, his face flushed and his hands clenched in tight fists.

Wes sat up as Mr. Zeller's son flew past and disappeared around the corner.

How had they grown so far apart? Bad patterns and old hurts had a way of tearing down relationships. He'd seen it before. His shoulders drooped as he soaked in the weight of the conflict he'd just observed. He sent off a brief prayer that they'd find a way to work through their differences and restore their relationship.

Wes was painfully aware of the importance of home and family. He'd lost his parents during his junior year in college, when their car skidded off the road and hit a tree in a fierce thunderstorm. Even though he and his parents shared a strong faith, giving him the hope of seeing them again, it had still been a painful time. His younger sister Jennifer had suffered the most, and she had no faith in God to help her cope.

And what had he done since his release to help his sister? Nothing. He had avoided her and left her wondering why. Wes closed his eyes, trying to blot out the painful situation from his mind. He should call her. But how could he answer her questions about all that had happened when he didn't understand it himself?

What would his parents have thought of his arrest and imprisonment and the choices he'd made? They might have been disappointed by his lack of courage, but they would have forgiven him and welcomed him home. He felt certain of that.

Rubbing his bare chin, he blew out a slow breath. Perhaps if his mom and dad were still alive he wouldn't have wandered halfway across Europe and the Northeast looking for a place to call home.

Memories from his childhood flooded his mind—happy times they had shared watching movies in the family room or simply sitting around the dinner table, talking about their day. And his parents always went out of their way to make holidays special, filled with fun and laughter.

The truth hit his heart. Home wasn't just a house where you stored your possessions. It was a place where loving relationships created strong bonds that couldn't be broken.

How could he make his way back to relationships like that and find a place to call home?

Chapter Seven

Lauren opened the heavy glass door of the Wild River Ski Lodge and slipped inside. The smell of French fries, hot chili and soggy woolen clothing greeted her. Pulling off her gloves, she tucked them in her pockets and glanced around, trying to calm her jumpy stomach. The fresh snowfall and school closings had drawn a large crowd to the mountain.

Lauren scanned the lobby, looking for Wes, but she didn't see her tall friend anywhere. A smile tugged at her lips. After his three-day visit to Long Meadow, she no longer thought of him as a stranger, but as a friend.

The smell of wood smoke and toasting marshmallows drew her toward the large fireplace at one end of the lobby. She loosened the plaid scarf around her neck and unbuttoned her coat.

See, I can come to Wild River just like everyone else. What happened here is in the past. I can let it go and move on. There's nothing to be afraid—

Someone tapped her on the shoulder. "Lauren? Is that you?"

She spun around and her breath caught in her throat. A tidal wave of emotion rolled through her, turning her knees to Jell-O and her mouth to parched cotton. For a second she thought she'd seen a ghost, but instantly she realized her mistake. "Ryan?"

He grinned and nodded. "It's been a long time."

"What are you doing here?" she whispered.

He chuckled. "Now that's not a very nice way to greet an old friend. My family owns Wild River, remember?"

"Of course I remember." The amusement in his eyes only upset her more. How could he greet her so calmly? He'd been there the night his brother—

She mentally slammed that door shut, refusing to let her thoughts carry her back there.

"You look great." His appreciative gaze traveled over her face and hair. "So you want to go over to the café and grab some lunch? My treat. We could catch up on old times."

Panic rose in her throat, choking off her voice. "No, I have to go." She whirled away from him.

"Lauren, wait. You don't have to be afraid of me."

Turning to face him, she jammed her hands in her coat pockets to hide their trembling. "I'm not afraid. I'm meeting someone."

Ryan crossed his arms, looking confused and a little hurt. "You heard what happened to my brother, didn't you?"

"Yes, I'm sorry," she whispered, barely able to

speak. Stephen had stolen so much from her, but she never wished him dead.

Ryan leaned toward her. "Listen, I know things sort of got…out of hand the last time you were with Stephen, but he never meant to hurt you. I hope you know that."

Almost seven years had passed since that night. Hot tears stung her eyes as she tried to decide what to believe. Stephen's death didn't erase his responsibility for what he'd done. She wouldn't stand there and let his brother say it didn't matter.

"He liked you, Lauren. He told me he called you, but your aunt said you'd already gone back to college."

Lauren conjured up a blurry image of Stephen Zeller. Handsome, athletic and the oldest son of the wealthy Zeller family, she'd had a secret crush on him since high school, naively believing a relationship with him would fill the longings in her heart. It didn't matter that he ran with a fast crowd that drank, raced cars on icy roads and pulled wild stunts on the slopes.

When he asked her out during spring break in her junior year in college, she'd almost had a heart attack. A quiet, artistic loner like Lauren didn't get asked out too often, especially not by someone like Stephen Zeller. Longing to be accepted by Stephen and the popular crowd who skied all day and partied all night, she said yes. Stephen swept her off her feet that week, but she soon learned he was self-serving and manipulative and only had one goal in mind.

"You're not still mad about what happened, are you?" Ryan asked, looking incredulous. "That was so long ago."

She clenched her hands into fists, fighting the urge to slap his face. "I made some foolish choices when I dated Stephen, but he took advantage of me in the worst way."

"Come on, Lauren."

She gulped in a breath. "I don't want to talk to you about old times or anything else. Don't even try to pretend we're friends. Stay away from me!"

His shocked expression quickly changed to one of stormy anger.

Dread rolled through Lauren. The Zeller family held more power and influence in the community than anyone else, and they were known for getting even for every insult.

Lord, please get me out of here before I say anything else. Spinning away from him, she dashed toward the door.

Wes stood and reached across the desk to shake Mr. Zeller's hand. "Thanks for your time, sir."

"You're welcome." The owner of Wild River Ski Resort rose to his feet and walked around to the front of his large wooden desk. "As I said, the only thing I have open right now is that part-time position in the Nature Center. With your experience and education, I'm not sure that would be right for you." Glancing toward the window, he paused for a moment. "Of course that position could become full-time in the spring. Let me give this some more thought and speak to some people. I'll get back to you in a few days."

Wes nodded, making an effort not to show his disappointment. "That'll be fine. You can leave a message with Bill Morgan. He'll know how to reach me."

"All right. I'll be in touch."

"Thanks." Wes picked up his coat from the back of the chair and left the office.

Arthur Zeller appeared friendly. But Wes suspected that behind his smile, he possessed a controlling nature and didn't like to be crossed. Working for him would be a challenge. Wes shook his head. Why was he worried? He didn't even have the job yet.

The buzzing conversation of the lunchtime crowd drifted toward Wes as he walked into the lobby. His mind shifted back to Lauren. Would she be open to him staying at Long Meadow a little longer? Bill had invited him to move in and share his small house as soon as his out-of-town guests left next week. Pleasant memories of the previous three days at Long Meadow rose in his mind.

Scanning the room, he searched for Lauren. He spotted her near the fireplace, engaged in conversation with a man. He caught sight of the man's profile and surprise rippled through him. Ryan Zeller leaned toward Lauren, an intense expression on his face.

Wes frowned. Something didn't look right. Ryan stood too close, and Lauren's posture looked rigid. Without warning, she spun away and ran toward the exit, anguish etched on her face.

Alarm jolted Wes into motion. Pushing through the crowd, he hustled after her. As he dashed out the door, he saw her cross the front drive and head for the parking lot.

"Lauren!" His shout echoed off the lodge's stone wall and faded into the cold, dry air. She didn't slow down or look back. He charged down the steps and ran after her, crossing the slushy drive. Concern spurred him on. If she didn't slow down, she'd slip and break her neck.

"Hey, what's your hurry?" he called.

Lauren reached her car only a few seconds ahead of him. Pulling her keys from her coat pocket, she sorted through them with a trembling hand. He stepped up beside her and she hurriedly brushed the tears from her cheeks.

His heart twisted as he watched her. "What happened in there?"

"It's nothing. I'm okay." She fumbled with her key, her voice shaking even more than her hands.

"Here, let me get it." He reached for the keys and unlocked the car door for her.

She lifted her gaze and the pain he read there tore a searing path to his heart. Anger rose and swirled through him. For a moment he considered charging back inside so he could shake Ryan Zeller until his teeth rattled. But what good would that do? Life wasn't fair. People hurt other people. He couldn't change that.

From his time in the Middle East he'd learned the wisdom of leaving tough situations in the hands of God. He alone was wise and powerful enough to balance the scales of justice and take care of revenge.

Wes wished he could share his thoughts with Lauren, but this wasn't the right time. Caring silence and waiting until she was ready to talk would probably mean more to her now.

"Do you want me to drive?" he asked.

"Okay, thanks." She stepped back from the open car door and looked up at him. Her nose glowed bright pink, and tears glistened on her eyelashes and her cheeks.

He resisted the urge to reach out and brush the tears away. Instead, he took her arm, walked her around to the other side of the car and opened the door for her. After he was sure she was settled, he closed the door and strode back to the driver's side.

He wished she would tell him what had happened with Ryan Zeller, but her hesitation made sense. She probably didn't consider their friendship deep enough for that…. Not yet.

Until then, he would do whatever he could to prove he was a friend worthy of her trust and confidence. Maybe that would open the door to what remained hidden in her heart.

Chapter Eight

Frightening questions cycled through Lauren's mind as she and Wes drove back to Long Meadow. What was Ryan Zeller doing back in Tipton? She had heard he lived in New York City and rarely visited his family. What would she do the next time she saw him? And what would happen when he saw Toby? The family resemblance was strong, and Ryan was one of the only people who knew what had happened that night.

Closing her eyes, she tried to calm her racing thoughts. The Lord had led her back home to Tipton. It couldn't be a mistake. She had prayed long and hard before making the move. Her aunt needed her. And Lauren needed a place to build a stable life for herself and Toby. But with Ryan back in town, would that be possible?

She opened her eyes and glanced at Wes. He sat beside her in the driver's seat, handling her car and the snowy roads with quiet confidence. Gratefulness rose in her heart. He hadn't pressed her to explain her tears. His caring response and willingness to drive her home sent a comforting wave of relief through her. Her tense shoulders relaxed and the storm in her heart began to subside.

Ten minutes later, they arrived at Long Meadow. Lauren asked Wes to park by the barn. Grabbing the sack from the back seat, she climbed out and shut her door.

"The tools are in here," she said as they waded through the deep snow. She slid open the heavy barn door and Wes followed her inside.

She flipped on the light and led Wes across the rough, wooden-plank floor toward the back corner of the barn.

"Wow, this is great."

Lauren glanced over her shoulder. Wes had stopped to admire the barn's large, open interior. An appreciative smile lit up his face as he looked up and turned full circle.

His response lifted her dismal spirits and shifted her focus to the future home of her gallery. "I've always loved this old barn, even when it housed our cows and was full of cobwebs and dusty hay. I used to swing from the loft on a big rope." She pointed to the open second floor that would soon be enclosed. She planned to use that area to show antique bedroom furniture, trunks and quilts. "In the summer, I'd beg to sleep up there."

Wes smiled and slipped his hands in his jacket pockets. "This is going to be a beautiful place."

"Thanks. There's still a lot to do, but we'll get there." Opening the gallery had been a long-standing dream, and she could easily imagine the rooms filled with treasured antiques and handcrafted works of art.

"Looks like you put in new electric and heat." He pointed toward the open-framed walls with multiple wires and vents still exposed.

She nodded. "New windows and plumbing, too. Now I need to Sheetrock and tape the walls. After that, there's just the painting and a few odds and ends. Then I can start moving in." Her summary didn't sound too daunting, but she knew it would take several more weeks of hard work before she could open the gallery.

"You're a pretty handy lady," he said, lifting his gaze to the open rafters and unfinished ceiling.

"I didn't do it all myself. But I have learned how to swing a hammer and use a circular saw."

He walked over to the closest wall and ran his hand down one of the two-by-fours, examining the framing. "It looks like you're doing a fine job."

Gratitude for his words warmed her heart. "Thanks."

"So when do you plan to open the gallery?"

"I don't know. It's taking a lot longer than I expected. People keep putting me off. I've been waiting more than two weeks for some guys to come put up that Sheetrock." She motioned toward the pile of building materials stacked near the front door. "If it wasn't so heavy, I'd do it myself."

Wes turned toward her. "I've worked with Sheetrock before. I could help you."

"But what about your job at Wild River?"

"I won't have an answer about that for a few days, and hanging out with Bill isn't an option. His sister and brother-in-law are visiting him till next week."

She certainly could use the help, but he'd already done so much. It wouldn't be right to take advantage of him. But what if she hired him? That made sense.

"Okay. You've got the job," she said with a little nod.

"I don't want you to pay me," he said swiftly, looking offended.

"You can't work for free. That wouldn't be fair."

Wes rubbed his chin and glanced at the pile of Sheetrock. "Tell you what, I need a place to stay until Bill's sister leaves, and you have a stalled project. How about we swap my labor for room and board?" He lifted his brows, waiting for her answer.

She glanced around the barn, feeling torn. This morning she'd thought it best for him to move on…but now his offer to help changed things. Perhaps his kindness had softened her heart, as well. But would it be wise to let him stay on at Long Meadow? Working with a handsome, caring man like Wes could be a problem. She knew what a fool she'd been where men were concerned. She'd have to be on guard to keep from indulging in foolish, romantic fantasies.

But how could she work with him every day and pretend she wasn't attracted to him? Lauren silently scolded herself. Fairy-tale romances with happily-ever-after endings only happened in novels or the movies…never in real life, especially hers.

Wes crossed his arms. "I'm not sure when I'll have an answer about the job at Wild River, so I don't know if I can put up all this Sheetrock, but I'll give it my best shot."

His sincere expression erased the last of Lauren's doubts. "Okay, you've got a deal."

Chapter Nine

Wes backed through the heavy barn door, his arms filled with broken and sawed-off pieces of Sheetrock. Stepping outside, he heaved them into the large blue trash can. The brisk air felt great after working in the dusty barn for the past few hours.

"Hold the door, here's some more." Lauren hustled toward him with another load of construction debris.

"Right this way." He stood back and grinned as she passed by. A fine layer of white Sheetrock dust covered her face and the blue bandanna she wore over her hair. Several curly wisps had escaped to frame her face. Even though she wore an old blue sweatshirt and well-worn jeans speckled with pale yellow paint, she was the prettiest assistant he'd ever worked with on a construction project. Distractingly pretty. But his attraction to Lauren was based on more than the physical.

Despite her petite size, Lauren possessed more energy and determination than many of his missionary teammates. He chuckled softly as he considered how much he enjoyed working with her.

Well, there had been that initial struggle the first hour as they silently tried to determine who would lead. When his greater construction skills became obvious, she'd given over leadership, though he could tell it had been a challenge for her.

Lauren tossed her pile into the nearly overflowing trash can and sent a cloud of chalky dust flying into the air. She coughed and waved her hand over the can, dispersing the haze. "Looks like that can's about full. I better roll it out to the road. Tomorrow's trash day."

"I'll get the other one." Wes grabbed the handle of the second can and pushed it down the drive with Lauren. The frozen ruts and icy gravel made it a challenge to steer the bulky cans, but Lauren shoved hers toward the road with tenacity. Wes slowed to match her steps. No need to rub in the fact that his long legs could easily outpace hers. She took pride in her ability to partner with him in the renovation work, and he saw no reason to discourage her.

With a final push, Lauren parked the trash can to the right of her rural mailbox and stood aside as Wes maneuvered his next to hers. Though no more snow had fallen since that first night Wes had stayed at Long Meadow, high piles deposited by the snowplow still lined the road. Shredded brown maple leaves and muddy gravel from the roadway had mixed in, staining the once-pristine piles.

Lauren glanced at her watch. "Toby should be home by now." Lifting her hand to shade her eyes against the low winter sun, she scanned the quiet country road.

"I'm sure his bus will be along soon." Wes hoped his words would ease the concern she always seemed to carry for her son. He brushed his dusty hands on his pants, intrigued once again by the bond between Lauren and Toby.

Spending time with Lauren and watching her interact with her son moved him in a way he hadn't expected. The bond they shared touched a place deep within and stirred up a longing he hadn't even known was there. He smiled, picturing Toby. Who could resist a little guy with a wide, toothless grin, tousled hair and an attraction to all things creepy, crawly and wiggly? If he ever had a son, he hoped he would be much like Toby.

A silver SUV pulled around the curve and slowed as it approached. Lauren waved and the car stopped. A young woman with short, light brown hair and bright blue eyes rolled down her window.

"Hey, Lauren." The woman's gaze shifted from Lauren to Wes and back with a slight lift of her brows. "What have you been up to? Seems like I haven't seen you in weeks."

"I've been working on the barn." Lauren smiled, leaning toward the open window. "Where are you headed?"

"I'm dropping off a meal for Charlene Hawkins. Did you hear she had a baby boy Tuesday night?"

"That's great. What did they name him?"

"Jonah Michael. Isn't that sweet?" The woman's gaze drifted toward Wes again. She smiled, obviously waiting to be introduced.

"Oh, this is Wes Evans." Lauren glanced his way. "He's a friend of Bill Morgan, and he's giving me a hand putting up Sheetrock in the barn."

"Nice to meet you, Wes. I'm Julia Berkley. You must be new in the area." Before he could comment, she continued. "I'm in real estate. Let me give you my card. I can help you with renting or buying." She reached into her large, brown leather purse on the seat beside her and retrieved her business card. Smiling, she leaned over and held it out the window toward him. "So you're a friend of Bill's?" Her eyes sparkled with interest as she asked the question.

"Yes. We've been friends since college."

"Bill and I go to Tipton Community Church," Julia said and then shot a flustered glance at Lauren. "And Lauren goes there, too, of course."

Wes nodded and held back a smile. Bill hadn't mentioned dating anyone. He'd have to ask Bill about Julia and see if he got the same rise in interest she showed.

"Well, I better run. I want to see that baby, and I have to get back home in time to put the frosting on my carrot cake before the potluck." Julia narrowed her eyes at Lauren. "You are coming tonight, aren't you?"

Lauren bit her lip and glanced down the road. "I'm not sure. I haven't talked to Tilley about it, and I don't know how much homework Toby has."

"Lauren, it's the weekend. And Wes needs to

come and meet everyone." Julia smiled at Wes. "She works too hard. Make her hang up the hammer and come."

A wave of uneasiness rippled through him. Meeting new people always opened up the possibility that someone would recognize him and ask questions about his imprisonment. Or they might not say anything but decide to tell someone connected with the media where to find him. That would put an end to his peaceful seclusion. He'd have to leave.

"Come on, Lauren, you know how much fun the potluck will be," Julia continued. "And the food is to die for." The second half of her statement she directed to Wes. "Mary Beth is bringing her maple-cured baked ham, and Elizabeth Stockwell is making her chocolate pecan cheesecake."

Wes's mouth began to water. They'd worked all afternoon without a break. His neck and shoulders ached, and he felt as hungry and thirsty as a nomad who'd been wandering in the desert for a few days. Maybe going along wouldn't be such a bad idea. Surely he could avoid answering too many questions if he was busy eating ham and cheesecake and spending time with Lauren and Toby.

Lauren's expression softened. "What time's the potluck?"

"Seven o'clock at the Community House." Julia grinned. "So you'll come?"

Lauren nodded. "Sure. We'll be there." Her glance darted toward Wes and she sucked in a quick breath. "I mean Toby and I will be there. You can do whatever you want." Her hands fluttered like a bird frightened from a bush. "Of course, you're welcome to come with us if you'd like, but you don't have to. If you'd rather stay home, that's fine, too. I'm sure Tilley could whip up something for dinner."

Lauren's flustered expression and sputtering comments made him smile. "The potluck sounds great. I wouldn't miss it."

Chapter Ten

Lauren took a sip of hot cider, leaned back in the metal folding chair and let her gaze travel around the busy Community House meeting room.

There had been a few surprised looks when she'd introduced Wes, but no one said anything unkind or made her feel uncomfortable. On the contrary, this whole evening had filled her with a warm sense of belonging. This was her town, and these were her neighbors and friends. It was time she stopped being such a recluse and got involved with people again.

"How do you ladies like my baked beans?" Bill Morgan, Wes's friend and the head naturalist at Wild River Nature Center, grinned across the table at Lauren and Julia. His blue eyes glowed as he waited for their answer. He had the lean build of a runner and wore his dark, wavy hair long enough to touch his collar in the back.

Lauren smiled and shook her head. Bill could never be accused of being shy and reserved. His quirky smile and wry sense of humor had entertained them all evening.

Julia beamed him a radiant smile. "They're delicious, Bill."

Lauren couldn't understand why Bill didn't pick up on Julia's obvious interest and ask her friend out. If he thought he'd wait for someone more interesting and attractive than Julia to come along, he'd be waiting a very long time.

Lauren reminded herself it was none of her business. What did she know about relationships, anyway? She shifted her thoughts to Bill's question. Rolling a bite around on her tongue, she tried to discern what he'd put in his recipe to give it that unique flavor. The beans were both sweet and tangy but also carried a hint of some ingredient she couldn't quite identify.

"Okay, what's your secret?" Lauren asked.

He leaned back in his chair, looking pleased. "I use real maple syrup and bake them overnight in a special ceramic pot."

"Overnight? Wow, I'm impressed." Lauren laid her fork across her plate and pushed it away, ruminating about her lack of skill in the kitchen. She'd been so busy working and caring for Toby she hadn't taken time to learn how to cook more than a few basic recipes.

Her cooking would never impress a man. She tried to squelch that depressing thought. It didn't matter. No one had asked her out in a long time.

Maybe it was because she gave off a silent message that said, "Don't ask. I'm not interested."

Until this past week.

Her wistful gaze drifted across the room, seeking Wes. She spotted him in line at the buffet table, helping Toby spoon something onto his plate. She chided herself and turned away to focus on Bill and Julia's conversation.

"Could you give me cooking lessons?" Lauren asked.

"What are you talking about? Your lasagna was great. I had seconds."

"Tilley made it. The cookies, too." Lauren sighed, picked up one of Tilley's perfectly round, oatmeal chocolate-chip cookies and took a bite. It melted in her mouth, leaving the delicious taste of milk chocolate lingering on her tongue.

"So where did you get your secret baked-beans recipe?" Julia asked.

"I don't know if I should tell you."

"Come on, Bill," Julia pleaded.

"All right. I got it from the newspaper."

Julia gasped and gave him a playful slap on the arm. "So, the great chef gets his recipes from the *Valley News?*"

"There's no shame in that. I think I'll call and get a subscription," Lauren added. "I need to learn how to cook now before it becomes a permanent handicap."

She looked up as Wes and Toby returned to the table. Greeting them with a smile, she helped Toby climb into his chair and scoot closer. Toby had chosen bright green Jell-O, several little fish-shaped crackers and a big scoop of macaroni salad. Those weren't exactly healthy choices, but she decided to let it go. He looked so happy. Besides, she didn't want to embarrass Wes. He'd volunteered to supervise Toby's trip back to the buffet table, and Lauren hadn't given any instructions.

She glanced at Wes's plate with an amused grin. He had heaped it full of baked ham, scalloped potatoes, seven-layered salad and green-bean casserole. On top of that mountain, he had balanced a homemade buttered roll. His second. After watching him eat for more than a week, it still amazed her that he could regularly consume such large quantities of food. He did work hard, but she decided he must also have a very high metabolism because he certainly wasn't overweight. In fact, he was in great shape.

Bill eyed Wes's plate. "Did you leave any food up there for me?"

"There's a little left. But you might want to hold off on thirds. They're starting to bring out the desserts."

Bill grabbed his plate and stood up. "Thanks for the warning. I'll check it out."

Wes turned to Lauren. "I can keep an eye on Toby if you'd like to go."

"Thanks, but I'm full."

"Mom, can *I* get some dessert?" Toby leaned toward her.

"What about all that food on your plate?"

"I'll eat it. I promise. I just want to get a chocolate doughnut before they're all gone."

Lauren looked from her eager son to his half-full plate. She knew they'd pay for it later tonight if he ate too much. "You've already had firsts and seconds."

Julia stood up and squeezed her shoulder. "It won't hurt him, Lauren. Every growing boy needs a chocolate doughnut once in a while. Let me take him."

Lauren sent her son a serious look. "All right, but only one doughnut."

Toby smiled, jumped out of his chair and took Julia's hand.

Wes chuckled. "Toby has a good appetite."

"All these choices would tempt anyone." Lauren's gaze lingered on Wes's face. Once again, she wondered about the scar on his left cheek. Had he played a rough sport like football or been in some kind of accident? The jagged red line didn't look old and faded, more like a recent injury. She considered asking him about it but decided to wait. Tonight she sensed a special closeness between them, and she didn't want to spoil the evening by asking too many questions. Why bring up the past? It didn't really matter, did it?

Looking beyond Wes's shoulder, Lauren noticed the front door swing open. A man in a black leather jacket stepped inside the Community House. Ryan Zeller. Her stomach lurched. She quickly turned and searched for Toby. She spotted him at the dessert table, still holding Julia's hand. Anxiety zinged along her nerves and she fought to think clearly.

Ryan crossed the room, scanning the crowd. She

knew the exact moment recognition flashed in his eyes. Changing course, he made his way directly toward her.

She moaned softly and rubbed her forehead. What would she say? How could she keep him from seeing Toby and making the connection to his brother? What if he said something about what had happened with Stephen in front of Wes or her son? Shame swept through her.

"Lauren, what's wrong?" Wes laid his hand on her arm.

She lowered her hand and focused on the man standing behind Wes.

"Hey, Lauren. Nice to see you again." Ryan's smile revealed perfectly even, white teeth, but it looked as false as a theatrical mask.

Wes turned. His expression became guarded as his intense gaze traveled over Ryan. A silent challenge seemed to pass between the two men as they assessed each other for a long moment. Then Wes glanced back at her.

She finally found her voice. "Wes, this is Ryan Zeller. Ryan, Wes Evans."

Wes didn't extend his hand. He simply crossed his arms and nodded.

Ryan rocked back on his heels, grinning. "So, Wes, what's your connection to this lovely lady?"

Lauren raised her chin and spoke before Wes had a chance. "Wes is helping me with renovations at Long Meadow."

Ryan lifted his eyebrows. "That's right. I heard you had someone living out there with you."

Heat flooded Lauren's face. She glanced at Wes.

The muscles in his jaw twitched, and he regarded Ryan with a steely gaze.

"I also heard you're opening a gift shop," Ryan added.

Was he purposely baiting her? Did he hope she would blow up and make a fool of herself? Lauren straightened her shoulders. "I'm opening an antique and art gallery."

"Sorry. My mistake," Ryan said with an amused expression.

Her anger bubbled nearer the surface, and she felt her neck and face flush. Flipping a long strand of hair over her shoulder, she glared at him.

"Hey, you don't have to get all hot and bothered." He reached out and ran his fingers down her cheek. "But you do look awfully pretty when you're mad."

She pulled in a startled breath and drew back.

Wes rose and towered over Ryan, shielding Lauren like a protective wall. "I think this conversation is over."

"Mommy, look what I got." Toby appeared at her side, holding out his dessert plate.

Lauren's stomach took a dive.

"Mommy?" Ryan stepped to the right and looked past Wes at Toby. He quickly shifted his gaze to Lauren. "I didn't know you had a son."

All the air seemed to deflate out of Lauren's lungs. Toby and Ryan stared at each other with large, blue-gray eyes that were almost identical. Their fine, silky hair was the same shade of blond.

Did Ryan see the resemblance? How could he miss it? Would he destroy her now by announcing it to Toby and everyone else?

Wes turned toward her son, blocking Ryan's view. "Come here, Toby. Let's see what you've got." He leaned down and checked out the pile of desserts on her son's plate. "Now I distinctly remember your mom saying only one dessert. How about I help you out by eating that big brownie?"

Toby giggled and offered the plate to Wes. "Okay, I brought the extra ones to share, but save that doughnut for me." Wes smiled at him and set the plate on the table. Then he stepped over and helped Toby climb in his chair.

Questions filled Ryan's eyes as he glanced from Lauren to Toby. He slipped his hands in his jacket pockets. "It looks like we have a lot more to talk about." With one last look at her son, he turned and walked away.

Lauren released a slow, shaky breath.

Wes sat down and turned to her. "Old friend?" Gentle concern filled his voice.

"That's not exactly how I'd describe him. We went to school together. His family owns Wild River."

She lifted her cup and took another sip of cider, avoiding Wes's gaze. Part of her longed to tell him everything, but she wasn't sure she had the courage. She liked Wes, and she was just beginning to hope he might be interested in her, too. But what would he think if she told him her connection to the Zeller family? That thought sent a sickening wave of shame rolling through her. Why would a spiritually mature man like Wes be interested in someone who had a past like hers?

She hated the way guilt and secrecy sapped the joy from her life. She knew the Bible said God would forgive any sin, but whenever she remembered the foolish choices she'd made and the consequences they had brought to her life, grief overwhelmed her. She longed to go back and make different choices that didn't leave her feeling demoralized and desolate. But that was impossible now.

Later that evening, Wes pulled into the driveway at Long Meadow and parked Lauren's car next to Tilley's old green Chrysler Valiant. He glanced in the back seat where Toby slept, quietly covered by a plaid blanket Lauren had tucked around him before they'd left the potluck. Lauren made no move to get out of the car, so he pulled up the brake and left the motor running to give them some heat.

He turned toward her. The moonlight reflected off the snow and painted the soft curves of her face with silver-blue shadows.

"Thanks for driving," she said, smiling across at him. "My depth perception at night is terrible. I think I need new contacts."

"I didn't know you wore contacts." He grinned, warmed by the fact he knew something else rather personal about her. The more time they spent together, the more he discovered. She was a woman of many layers, and she was only beginning to allow him a peek past the surface.

She laughed softly. "I'm almost blind without them."

"Just let me know next time you need a chauffeur."

"Wes, can I ask you something?"

Her serious tone made him uneasy, but he forced a smile. "Sure."

"How come you don't have a car?"

Cold air seeped down his neck and he shivered. He knew something like this was coming. What did he expect? How long could their friendship continue to grow without her wondering why he owned nothing but a steel-framed backpack, and never talked about the past few years of his life? Did he expect she'd never ask questions and just be willing to accept him as a man with no past and no possessions?

He rubbed his cold hands together while he searched for a plausible answer. "I've worked in a lot of different places, so I haven't owned a car for a while."

One look in her eyes and he knew he hadn't fooled her. The disappointment on her face hit him hard. He deserved it. How could he expect Lauren to trust him if he wasn't willing to share more about himself than that? He'd have to risk telling her a few things or their friendship was doomed, and he was beginning to believe that would be a fate worse than telling her the truth.

"My last car was a great little Volkswagen. It had over a hundred thousand miles and still purred like a kitten." He smiled, remembering his well-loved car. "I bought it from one of my coworkers, and even though it had a few problems, it kept going like it had nine lives."

"What happened to it?"

He rubbed his chin and blew out a deep breath. "Someone stole it." That was the truth, though it wasn't the whole story. Government officials opposed to his missionary work had confiscated everything he owned. None of it had ever been returned. He'd lived a simple life, but it still bothered him that he'd lost his computer, his car and a few other personal possessions. When he left prison and flew out to Turkey and on to Switzerland, all he had were the clothes on his back, his journal and his Bible.

Lauren clicked her tongue. "Oh, that's terrible."

"Yeah, I hated losing that car. I felt like I'd lost an old friend."

"And you never got it back?"

"Nope." He was surprised by the empathy in her eyes. "It's okay. I'll get another car as soon as I get a job."

"But you sound pretty attached to your old car."

Wes smiled. "The only things holding it together were prayer and a few little automotive repair tricks I learned from my friend Raheem."

Lauren laughed softly. "You are a man of many talents."

"Right." He drew the word out in a cynical tone. Nagging doubts surfaced again. What would he do if the job at Wild River didn't work out? Would he have to leave Vermont? All his education and training had focused on preparing him to be a missionary. He hoped some of those skills would transfer to the secular workplace, but he wasn't so sure now.

Would he be able to earn enough money to support himself? When would he be in a secure financial position and have something to offer Lauren?

No, he wouldn't go there.

Shaking off those disturbing questions, he focused on Lauren. But the sweet concern in her eyes sent those thoughts circling through his mind again.

He was a fool for even considering the possibility of a relationship with Lauren. She needed someone strong and stable with courage and a firm faith, not a man who carried a load of regrets and an empty wallet.

Chapter Eleven

Lauren heard Toby's rippling laughter echo up the stairs, followed by Wes's deep chuckle. Curious to find out what they were up to, she picked up the wicker laundry basket and headed down to the living room. A smile rose from her heart when she spotted her son dancing around the coffee table. Wes had pulled the navy-blue, high-backed chair up to the table so they could play a game of checkers. He sat there watching Toby, grinning like a man with a blissful secret.

"I jumped him! I jumped him!" Toby shouted when he saw her. "Now he has to crown me." Delight filled her son's eyes and an impish grin flooded his face. He loved games, and Lauren had played more rounds of Candy Land and Chutes and Ladders than she cared to count.

Wes clasped his hands and leaned forward, assessing the checkerboard. "I don't know what to do. Looks like you've got me now." He frowned, putting on a good show for her son. "I hope you'll have a little mercy on me. I haven't played checkers in a long time."

"No mercy, no mercy," her son chanted.

Wes looked up and sent Lauren a quick wink while Toby trooped around to his side of the coffee table and flopped down on the couch.

"Who taught you how to play checkers?" Wes asked, scrutinizing the board.

"My mom." Toby turned to her with a proud grin.

"Well, that explains it. No wonder you're winning." Wes slid one of his last three checkers in line for Toby to take another jump.

Toby hooted as he captured Wes's piece.

"Good move, Toby." Lauren smiled. Did Wes have any idea how much winning this simple game of checkers meant to her son? Yes, she knew he did. That's why he'd taken time to play. As she gazed at Wes, warmth and gratitude flowed through her, and the protective wall she'd tried to maintain around her heart crumbled a little more. She set her laundry basket on the floor and took a seat next to Toby on the couch.

"I got three kings, see?" Toby pointed to the board.

"Wow, that's great." Lauren tenderly ruffled his hair back off his forehead.

"I'm afraid he's gonna beat the pants off me," Wes said.

Toby folded over, giggling. Lauren lifted her brows and shot Wes a quick glance.

Wes grimaced and looked genuinely apologetic. "Sorry. My grandpa used to always say that whenever we played games. It's sort of an Evans family tradition."

Lauren nodded, suppressing a grin. It pleased her to hear him talk about his family.

"Come on, Wes, it's your turn," Toby urged. "You gotta hurry up and move so I can beat the pants off you!"

Lauren rolled her eyes but couldn't hold back her laughter this time. The phone rang. Wes sacrificed his second-last checker, and Lauren reached to pick up the receiver.

Wes's spirit deflated as he watched Lauren's warm response to the phone call. A little smile played at the corners of her lips as she pushed her hair over her shoulder and settled back on the couch. He had no clue who was on the other end of the line, but he had a sneaking suspicion it was a guy, and that bothered him.

"Okay, I promise." She laughed softly, then turned and held out the phone to him. "It's for you. It's Bill."

Relief washed over him and he silently scolded himself for feeling jealous. Lauren hadn't made any commitment to him. He had no right to hover over her or screen her phone calls, although he wished he could. He doused those thoughts and lifted the receiver to his ear.

"Hey, Bill." As he listened to his friend's greeting, he watched Lauren try to calm her son's wiggly protests over putting their checker game on hold.

"I heard from Arthur Zeller."

Bill's words caught Wes's attention.

"He said the job is yours," Bill added.

"That's great. When did he call?" Wes smiled at Lauren, anxious to tell her the good news.

She returned a tentative smile, reflecting curiosity.

"Just now," Bill said. "The Nature Center is closed Monday, so he wants you to start Tuesday morning."

"This Tuesday?" Wes frowned slightly and shifted his gaze away from Lauren. What about the work they had left to finish on the barn? The last thing he wanted to do was disappoint Lauren.

For a moment he considered turning down the job but immediately dismissed that idea. He had to start earning a living and get himself established or he'd never have anything to offer her. He frowned at his line of thinking.

"He said he can only give you part-time right now. I hope that's okay."

"Sure, that's fine." The pay wouldn't be much, but it was a start, and he'd still have time to work with Lauren.

"My sister and her husband are flying out Sunday. You can move in Monday morning if you're ready. But I sure wouldn't blame you if you wanted to stay at Long Meadow."

He stood and walked toward the front window. "Monday's fine. Thanks. I appreciate it."

Toby appeared at his side and tugged on his sleeve. "Come on, Wes, we've got to finish our game." Wes laid his hand on Toby's head and the boy gazed up at him with imploring eyes. The thought of moving to Bill's and not seeing Toby and Lauren every day twisted painfully through him, diluting the pleasure of learning about his new job.

Toby grabbed his hand and tugged him toward their game.

Lauren moved to intercept her son. "Toby, stop. He'll be off the phone in a minute."

Toby dropped Wes's hand and shuffled back toward the couch, looking dejected.

"Wes, are you there?" Bill asked.

"Sorry. What did you say?"

"I said I'm glad the job came through. That's an answer to prayer."

"I appreciate you putting in a good word for me. I'm sure that helped. Look, I've got to go. I'm in the middle of a game with Toby."

"Okay. Take care. I'll talk to you soon."

"Right. I'll give you a call." Wes pushed the Off button. He turned to Lauren. "I got the job at the Nature Center." He braced himself, expecting to see disappointment rise in her eyes.

She gasped and threw her arms around him. "Oh, Wes! You got the job!"

He pulled in a surprised breath, then laughed and hugged her back. It didn't last more than two seconds but was long enough to warm his heart and tighten his throat.

Lauren dropped her arms and stepped back, her face flushed, her eyes wide. "Sorry, I shouldn't have—"

"No, no, it's fine." He wished he could say how much her hug meant, but he couldn't think of how to put it without sounding like a fool.

"That means you're staying?" Toby asked.

Wes smiled and nodded.

"Wahoo!" Toby wrapped his little arms around Wes's legs in a powerful hug.

"Thanks, buddy." Wes tousled Toby's hair, then squatted down to the boy's eye level. "What I mean is, I'm staying in Tipton and working at the Nature Center, but I'll be living at Bill Morgan's house."

Toby's face puckered in a frown. "Why are you moving over there?"

"Bill and I are old friends, and he's offered me a place to stay."

"Can't you stay here? We don't want you to go."

A combination of tenderness and embarrassment flashed across Lauren's face. She laid her hand on her son's shoulder. "Toby—"

Wes held up his hand. "No, it's okay. Let me explain." He placed his hands on Toby's shoulders. "It's been great staying here with you and your mom and Tilley. But now I need to get settled and start my new job."

"But I like playing games with you and shoveling snow and fixin' the pipes."

"We've had some good times."

"Will you come back and see us?"

"Sure I will." He squeezed Toby's shoulder. "We

have to play checkers again so I can beat the pants off you."

Toby's grin resurfaced. "Okay."

Tilley leaned her head in from the kitchen. "Lauren, it's almost 10:30. Don't forget about the birthday party."

Toby gasped. "Mom, I can't miss Brandon's party!"

Lauren glanced at her watch. "It's okay, honey. You won't miss it. Run up and brush your teeth and wash your face. You still have some breakfast on your chin."

Toby dashed toward the steps and skidded across the hardwood floor in his stocking feet. Slowing at the bottom of the stairs, he turned back to them. "Hey, Wes, can we finish our game later?"

"I think we should just declare you the winner." Wes pointed toward the checkerboard. "You've got four kings and I've only got one piece left."

Toby grinned. "Okay. I'll be the winner."

Wes watched Toby run up the steps, but his thoughts quickly reverted to his phone conversation and new job.

"Are you moving over to Bill's today?" Lauren asked.

"No. His sister and her husband leave Sunday, so Bill said Monday would be best."

Stepping back, she nodded, disappointment shading her eyes. Was it because she'd lost her partner in the renovation work or for another reason?

"The job's only part-time," Wes added, hoping to ease her mind. "I'm sure I'll have time to come back and help you with the barn."

"You don't have to." Lauren glanced at him with cool detachment. "We had a deal. You worked in exchange for room and board. You don't need to—"

Frustration rose and tangled his thoughts. "Lauren, you know that's not why I helped you."

"It's not?" She lifted her brows with a disbelieving look, but it barely masked the pain of betrayal in her eyes.

"No." He struggled to put his thoughts into words. "I helped you because I wanted to, because we're friends."

"Really?" Her sarcastic tone surprised him.

Exasperated, he crossed his arms. "Yes, and friends help each other out when they need it. Do you have a problem with that?"

She didn't answer but bent and began tossing the checker pieces in the box.

"Let me do that," he said. "The loser is supposed to clean up. At least, that was always the rule at my house."

She continued sweeping pieces off the board as though she didn't hear him.

"Lauren, stop. Talk to me. Tell me what's wrong."

"Nothing. I'm just cleaning up. I have to take Toby to the party."

"Are you upset because I'm moving to Bill's?"

Her eyes flashed. "No, I don't care where you live."

Pain ricocheted through him. She didn't care? No, he didn't believe her.

He reached for her hands and lifted them away from the checkerboard. "Listen to me. I'm not running out on you and Toby. I want to help you. I'm going to see that job through." He looked into her eyes and willed her to hold his gaze. "But it's more complicated than that. I care about you…a lot. And that's why I think it's best if I move over to Bill's. But that doesn't mean we won't see each other. At least, I hope not." He smiled as he watched her expression change. "I'd like us to spend more time together…besides working on the barn."

Lauren bit her lower lip. "Wes, that's sweet…I'm sorry. I didn't mean to act like such a…oh, I don't know what's the matter with me."

He sighed and rubbed his thumbs over the tops of her hands. The story Lauren had related about her absent father ran through his mind, followed by un-answered questions about Toby's father. She had good reasons to distrust men. "It's all right. You're just being cautious. That makes sense."

"Well, it's been a long time since…. I'm scared, Wes. I don't even know what to say or how to do this." She looked up at him through her dark eye-lashes.

He smiled, touched by her honesty. "All I'm asking for right now is a chance to be your friend and get to know you better. Let's take it slow and keep talking. How does that sound?"

Slowly, she smiled, and her eyes shone. "That sounds good to me."

He squeezed her hands and let them go, although

he wished he could hug her again. But he intended to keep his word. Take it slow. Prove himself. Win her trust, and then maybe her heart.

Chapter Twelve

Lauren glanced across the glittering field of snow toward the tree-covered hills and azure sky beyond. The heavy snow painted the forest a frosty lavender and deep blue.

Gliding along the trail on cross-country skis, she looked over her shoulder. Wes struggled, trying to keep his skis untangled and master the rhythm that came so easily to her. She had to admire him for tackling a new sport on their first date.

Her heart felt like melted butter every time she remembered the sweet words he had shared with her that morning. Then he'd coaxed her away from the barn renovations and asked her to choose something for them to do together that afternoon.

Now she wondered if she'd made a wise choice. Most men didn't like to feel incompetent on a date. What about Wes? Would it spoil the day? She purposely slowed her pace.

"Hey, this isn't a race. Relax," she called, watching his determined expression and vigorous arm motions. "We're supposed to be having fun."

"I am having fun," he insisted, but his face was flushed and his forehead glistened. Looking up, he broke his stride. His long legs, poles and skis tangled. With a startled shout, he landed face first on the snowy trail.

She quickly skied to his side. "Wes, are you okay?" No answer. She knelt and touched his shoulder. A tremor shivered through her.

He groaned and raised his head.

She sucked in a quick breath, sympathy filling her heart. "Oh, Wes." His sunglasses had protected his eyes, but thick clumps of snow coated his entire face and hat like a frosty mask.

He rolled over and slowly sat up. "That was a crazy way to let you know I wanted to stop and take a break."

Relief washed over her and she stifled a giggle. He might have lost his balance but not his sense of humor.

He raised his sunglasses and squinted against the sun's bright reflection. Swiping at his face with his snow-covered gloves, he smeared the mess around.

"Here, let me help." She pulled off her bulky gloves and gently wiped the snow from his nose. Her finger lightly traced the jagged scar on his cheek as she brushed the snow away. The frozen flakes stung her fingers, but she flicked them off and continued.

"Sorry you took such a dive." A shiver passed through her as she whisked snow from his forehead.

He pulled off his gloves and shook the snow from them. "It's not your fault."

"But this was my idea."

"Yes, but I agreed."

She smiled, thankful he didn't seem upset with her.

His gaze shifted back to her and his dark eyes glowed with mischief and something else. "I'm glad you suggested cross-country skiing."

"You're a good sport to try it." She tenderly brushed the last of the snow from his chin, trying not to focus on her trembling hands or fluttering stomach.

"I'd fall on my face any day if it means I get this kind of personal attention." He chuckled, then his grin slowly melted away and tenderness filled his eyes. "Thank you, Lauren."

"For what?" she whispered, still kneeling in the snow beside him.

"For spending today with me."

She opened her mouth to speak, but her words disappeared like the snowflakes melting on her warm hand.

His gaze roamed her face, caressed her eyes, her cheeks, and stopped at her mouth. His serious, searching look made his intention clear. He wanted to kiss her.

Longing and fear swept through her as Wes slid his warm fingers down her cheek and cupped her chin in his hand. Leaning toward her, he whispered her name just as his lips brushed against hers. His kiss was tentative and achingly gentle as he waited for her response. Her emotions danced with delight.

A loud crash startled them. They pulled back.

"What in the world?" Wes turned and squinted toward the trees.

Lauren's heart raced. She forced herself to focus, searching for an explanation for the sound. "Maybe it was just a branch falling from the heavy snow." Scanning the snow-draped trees lining the trail, she saw a man in black shift into view from behind a maple trunk.

"Look over there." She pointed toward the woods. Was the man spying on them? Suddenly, he raised something black and metallic to his face and pointed it toward them. Lauren gasped. Her mind spun. Was it a gun? Binoculars? A camera?

Wes stiffened. "Hey! What do you think you're doing?" His angry words roared across the silent park and sent a frightening shudder through her. Jerking his boots from their bindings, he sprung to his feet and lunged through the deep snow, chasing the stranger farther into the trees.

"Wes, wait!" Panic shot through her, as she took off after him.

The man in black darted through the trees, a camera clearly swinging from his neck. He glanced over his shoulder, but his face was covered by a ski mask, making it impossible for Lauren to tell who he was.

"Wes! It's just a camera. Let him go."

Ignoring her plea, Wes plunged through the snowdrifts, yelling for the man to stop. Lauren's breath came in short gasps, and her side ached as she fought to catch up.

Why was Wes so upset? It didn't make sense. Who cared if someone took their picture? Of course it had been a rude interruption to their kiss, but Wes's angry response seemed totally out of proportion to the situation.

Suddenly, a sickening realization washed over Lauren. Her steps stalled. Wes didn't want anyone to see that kiss. The fact that a photographer had captured it on film had released this fury. Her stomach twisted into a tight knot. He must be hiding from someone—someone who would be hurt or angry about that kiss.

Before Wes could close the distance, the photographer scrambled over a snowbank to the plowed park service road and dashed off, disappearing around the bend.

Wes's shoulders sank. Panting, he kicked at the snow, then turned and trudged back toward her.

She froze, her heart pounding, her senses reeling.

"I can't believe he got away," Wes huffed.

She clamped her lips on her storming emotions. Bitter disappointment weighed her down as though she carried a sack of heavy stones on her back. What was Wes's excuse for his behavior? Could he be like all the other men in her life—untrustworthy, deceptive and self-serving?

Wes laid his sweater in his pack, folded his extra pair of jeans and set them on top. He grabbed his Bible and journal from the bedside table and tucked them in by his sweatshirt and clean socks. Tomorrow morning he'd leave Long Meadow.

Glancing around the bedroom he had called home for almost two weeks, defeat and loneliness welled up in his chest. Would he ever find a place where he could settle down in peace and not be haunted by his past?

Yesterday's confrontation with the photographer had ruined his time with Lauren and brought his worst fears to light. Even in this remote corner of Vermont, someone had tracked him down and threatened to destroy the fragile new life he wanted to build.

Of course, he could be wrong. Maybe that photographer didn't really know his identity and it was only a frightening coincidence. But Wes had been the first one up that morning so he could carefully scan the Sunday edition of the *Valley News*. When he didn't find a photo of him and Lauren or a story exposing his past, he wasn't sure if he should be relieved or more worried.

He rubbed his forehead. The thought of praying and bringing his hurt and confusion to the Lord came to mind, but once again, guilt and unanswered questions made that seem futile. What did he expect God to do? Turn back time? He had made his choice. Now he had to live with it.

Lauren had been painfully quiet and had avoided him ever since they'd returned from skiing yesterday afternoon. They'd gone to church this morning and they'd eaten lunch with her aunt and Toby, but she hadn't looked him in the eyes or spoken more than two or three words to him.

She probably thought he was a raving lunatic after watching him chase that photographer. She'd be better off without him. Why would she want to tie herself down to someone like him?

A knock sounded at his door. Wes hesitated, both hoping and dreading that it was Lauren. Explaining the whole situation seemed impossible. She thought he was crazy. Maybe that was better than telling her the truth.

"Come in," he called, resignation in his voice.

The door opened. Tilley stood on the threshold. "How's the packing going?" Her warm smile made her eyes crinkle at the corners.

"Okay." He avoided her gaze and continued adding the last few items to his pack.

"I'll be heading into town tomorrow morning around nine. I can take you over to Bill's then, if you like."

Wes nodded and forced a small smile. "Thanks."

"May I come in a minute?"

"Sure."

She sat in the brown overstuffed chair by the window.

"I've enjoyed getting to know you, Wes. I know Lauren and Toby have, too."

He sat on the side of the bed. "Thanks. You've all made me feel at home here." He couldn't keep the edge of sadness out of his voice.

"I'm sorry to see you go…especially with things so unsettled between you and Lauren."

He sat up straighter and searched her softly wrinkled face. How much had Lauren told her? Did she know about their kiss or the incident with the photographer? "What do you mean?"

"I may be old, but I'm not blind. Something must have happened yesterday between you and Lauren, and it's obviously still bothering both of you."

Wes started to protest, but Tilley lifted her hand. "I raised Lauren since she was a toddler and I know her better than anyone else does. She's a very special young woman with many fine qualities and talents, but she's been through a lot. Sometimes she can seem cold and standoffish, but she doesn't mean it. That's just how she tries to protect herself and Toby."

Wes nodded, sensing the truth in Tilley's words.

"George and I did the best we could to raise her, but she's always struggled over her father's decision to leave her here with us." Tilley lifted her silver brows and sent him a knowing look. "And then being a single mother and caring for her son all alone has been difficult, too."

Once again Wes felt the weight of Lauren's pain, even though he didn't know the details.

Tilley reached forward and patted his knee. "You're a good man, Wes. Lauren's come to care for you. And I thought I was beginning to sense you cared for her, too."

Wes had no idea his growing feelings for Lauren had been so obvious. "Well…I do…I mean, she's—"

Tilley smiled and dismissed his comments with a wave of her hand. "You don't have to explain yourself to me. Lauren's the one you should talk to. I just don't want you to take her response these past couple of days too seriously."

Confusion swirled through him as memories flashed in his mind—Lauren's laughter and dazzling smile as they played games with Toby, the look of trust in her eyes as he promised to return and help her finish the work on the barn, the kiss they had shared, and finally, the wall of silence and suspicion that had separated them since he'd chased off that photographer.

"I'm not sure how Lauren feels, but I don't want to hurt her or Toby. That's why I'm leaving."

She looked at him with a gentle, caring expression. "Is that the real reason?"

Guilt washed over him. Should he tell Tilley the whole story? It would be a huge relief to let someone else know the truth. He looked into Tilley's warm and wise eyes and knew he had found a friend who would listen without judging.

"I was a missionary…before I came here," Wes said slowly, then crossed his arms and frowned at the floor. "And I made some choices that…hurt others." A boulder he couldn't swallow lodged in his throat and his eyes burned. He had to wait a few seconds before he could continue. "I want to make a fresh start and build a new life. But every time I try, something happens and the past rises up to slap me in the face."

Tilley sat quietly for a moment. She didn't look the least bit surprised by his confession. "Unresolved issues have a way of doing that," she said gently.

"Yeah."

"It seems you still have some things to sort out."

"I suppose, but I'm not sure how. There's no way to go back and change what happened. That's impossible."

Sorrow rolled through him as he thought of the friends he had left behind in the Middle East. By helping him care for street children and listening to the Bible stories at the center, they had put themselves in jeopardy. The confession he had finally signed after sixteen months of beatings and interrogations had sealed their fate. He couldn't be certain what had happened to them, but the stories he'd heard filled him with grief and regret.

His silent plea flew toward Heaven. *Please, Father, don't let them suffer because of my failures and lack of faith.* He knew it was too late to change many of the painful events that had already taken place, but he couldn't help wishing there was a way.

"That's another reason I'm leaving." He focused on Tilley with new resolve. "I don't want to drag Lauren into the middle of this. It will be better for her if I just fade out of the picture."

"I'm not sure about that. Lauren's a young Christian…but she's seen God's faithfulness in her life, and that's given her some practical wisdom." Tilley smiled. "Talk to her, Wes. See if you can work this out."

"I appreciate what you're saying, but I don't want to complicate Lauren's life. She has enough to deal with right now." He sighed, feeling deflated.

How could he lay his burdens on her shoulders? Hadn't he been sent here to help her, not the other way around? He'd promised to be her friend, the one she could trust to help her overcome the sorrows of her past. But that kiss had changed everything. He'd crossed the line.

Lauren's sweet response replayed through his mind, stirring up longings for more than friendship. He slammed the door on those thoughts. No, he had to retreat to Bill's and find a way to deal with this on his own. But before he left, he owed Lauren an apology. That much was certain.

Chapter Thirteen

Lauren leaned against the front of the dryer, letting its gentle rumble and warmth soothe her aching muscles. Though two days had passed since she'd gone cross-country skiing with Wes, she still felt the effects of her outing. Unfortunately, it wasn't only her muscles that hurt. Wes's angry response to the mysterious photographer and his somber mood since then had bruised her heart.

She slowly sorted through a pile of Toby's socks, rolled up pairs as she found their mates and tossed them into the laundry basket.

Even socks have a match! Why didn't she? She huffed a disgusted sigh. This moping had to stop.

She glanced at her watch. Wes was leaving with Tilley soon, but it wasn't too late. She could still go to him and talk things over. There might be a chance to repair their friendship before he left.

No, there had been plenty of opportunities for

Wes to explain his actions if he wanted to, but he hadn't. There'd been no more talk about them working on the barn together or promises to call or see her again after he moved to Bill's—nothing but painful silence.

Of course, that wasn't entirely Wes's fault. She had avoided him like he had a contagious disease. This morning she'd skipped breakfast and had only seen him for a brief moment in the kitchen as she hurried Toby toward the door so he wouldn't miss his school bus.

Toby's tearful goodbye to Wes had just about done her in. But she'd hustled her son off without meeting Wes's gaze. Regret swirled through her now as she recalled the scene, stirring up a frightening mix of emotions in her heart. How could he say he cared about her and then leave without even saying goodbye? It served her right for opening the door to her heart too soon to a man she hardly knew.

"Lauren?" Wes ducked under the low doorway leading into the laundry room.

She gasped and dropped the socks she was rolling.

"Sorry, I didn't mean to surprise you." He hesitated there, his tall frame practically filling the doorway.

"No…it's okay." She snatched up the socks from the floor, her face flaming. "I just didn't hear you coming."

Wes glanced down at his heavy boots. "I wanted to talk to you before I go." His serious tone sent shivers down her back.

She pressed her lips together, steeling her heart. "Okay."

He looked at her with unmistakable tenderness. "I want to apologize for what happened on Saturday."

Hope rose in Lauren's heart. Maybe he'd finally offer some kind of explanation for his wild chase through the woods.

He stepped closer. "I'm sorry. I was way out of line."

She swallowed hard and nodded, still uncertain what exactly he was including in his apology.

Wes closed his eyes and shook his head. "What I mean is, I shouldn't have kissed you."

Those words tore through her, and she stared at him in stunned silence. Her knees felt like jelly, and she leaned against the dryer for support.

"I'm sorry, Lauren, I'm not explaining this very well. What I'm trying to say is…a kiss is special. It's like a promise. And it was wrong for me to take that from you without…" He blew out a shaky breath. "You should save your kisses for the man you're going to marry."

Lauren's heart lurched, and tears stung her eyes. She quickly blinked them away.

"Maybe after I work things out, we might be able to—"

She held up her hand. "No, it's okay. I understand." She didn't, but hearing him hold out some false hope for them to be together in the future hurt worse than the truth. Wes didn't love her. His kiss had only been an impulsive response to a romantic moment.

Wes looked hurt and a little bewildered. "I don't think you understand what I mean. I like you, Lauren—very much. That's not what this is about. There are some things I have to work out before I can get involved in a relationship."

She looked into his eyes, wishing with all her heart that the tender message she read there was true. But what was he really saying? Did he want her to wait or was he telling her goodbye?

"I don't know how you expect me to believe that when you act one way one day…and totally different the next. I don't know what to think."

He lowered his chin and nodded. "Yeah. This has all been a little confusing for me, too." Sincerity shone in his eyes. "I need some time to pray about everything and think things through. Could you give me that?"

Her first reaction was, *No, don't believe him. Don't promise him anything. You're a fool to hold on to any hope.* But her heart had already agreed. She nodded, unable to say the words.

"Thanks, Lauren." His gaze lingered and he looked as though he wanted to say more, but he turned away and disappeared through the kitchen door.

Wes stretched out on the bed in his room at Bill's and placed his hands behind his head. The heater made a soft ticking sound as the metal expanded and sent warmth into the room, but his nose and fingers still felt cold.

He could hear Bill taking a long shower in the

bathroom on the other side of the wall. His friend had a funny way of singing off-key while he was in there, but Wes didn't laugh. Nothing seemed humorous right now.

It had been four days since he'd seen Lauren—four of the most miserable days he'd experienced since he'd been in prison. He couldn't stop thinking about her or berating himself for kissing her and then leaving Long Meadow without explaining his past. That decision just seemed to confirm his lack of courage and unworthiness.

No photos or stories had appeared in the local paper. He'd overreacted to that photographer and jeopardized his friendship with Lauren for nothing.

He'd spent a lot of time praying, asking for direction. But the heavens seemed silent, and he felt weary from the inward battle. Closing his eyes, he tried to rest, but Lauren's image floated before him, her smile and soft blue eyes telling him things her words had not. The picture was so clear he felt like he could almost reach out and touch the gentle contours of her face and feel the warmth of her lips. Wes groaned and rolled over.

He had to stop this. There was no point in torturing himself by thinking about her. He didn't sense he had clear direction to move ahead, so that meant he should wait. And waiting had never been easy for him.

Opening his eyes, he focused on the night sky through the small window above his bed. A myriad of stars twinkled, sending a message back to him.

God was still in His Heaven, even if He was

silent. He had spoken volumes in other ways and at other times. He would speak again, if Wes was patient enough to wait and listen for His answer.

Father, I'm coming to You again, asking for wisdom. Please show me Your will. I know I rushed ahead and made a mess of things with Lauren. Show me what to do. Make it so clear I can't miss it. I don't want to hurt her. Most of all, please take care of her and give her everything she needs. And if that doesn't include me, then help me accept that and let her go.

Lauren gripped the phone more tightly and stared out the front window as she listened to Mrs. Barlow, Toby's teacher.

"Toby is not picking up the concepts he needs, and he's falling further behind every day. The year is half over and he's still not reading. And it certainly doesn't help that he's missed so much school."

Guilt rose and tightened Lauren's stomach. She'd let Toby stay home twice this week because he had complained of stomachaches. She didn't have the heart to send him to school when he seemed sick. He chewed his nails to the quick and looked close to tears on the mornings she did send him.

"I don't see any other alternative," Mrs. Barlow continued. "I'm recommending Toby be evaluated by the district special services team."

Lauren sank down on the couch. "Mrs. Barlow, Toby's been through a lot, what with the move and getting settled into a new home and school. Those aren't easy adjustments for any six-year-old to make, let alone a sensitive little boy like Toby. Don't you think you could just give him a little more time?"

"I understand his *situation*." His teacher's voice practically bristled with condescension. "But Toby's moodiness and erratic behavior is becoming more disruptive to the class, and that's on top of his struggles with reading. This past week has been especially difficult. We have to do something."

"But referring him for an evaluation seems a little extreme."

"Ms. Woodman, I believe your son has some serious issues that need to be addressed. You do want him to succeed in school, don't you?"

"Of course I want him to succeed. But he's only six years old. Children learn to read at different ages. Maybe he's just a late bloomer and all this pressure to keep up with the other children is what's making him have such a difficult time. I don't want him labeled."

Mrs. Barlow sniffed loudly. "The purpose of the evaluation would be to diagnose any learning disabilities or emotional issues that are making learning difficult for Toby. He would see a child psychologist, as well as people trained to evaluate his intelligence and learning difficulties. The benefits would far outweigh any possible negative impact from being diagnosed. I don't really think there's anything for you to be afraid of."

The woman's attitude and patronizing tone just about pushed Lauren over the edge. She took a deep breath before she answered. "I'm not ready to agree to an evaluation, but I'll think about it."

"Well, something has to be done about Toby."

"I understand what you're saying. I'll let you know my decision." Lauren hung up and leaned back on the couch. She closed her eyes and sighed with a weariness only another single parent could understand.

She knew this week had been difficult for Toby. It had been awful for her, too. She missed Wes, and she felt that might be part of her son's problem as well. All the more reason to stay away from him and protect Toby from any more disappointments.

But was that the right answer? Avoiding Wes hadn't resolved anything. It had made both her and Toby miserable, and Wes hadn't looked too happy when he'd left, either.

All week she'd had a nagging feeling that she hadn't handled things well. If she'd had the courage to ask Wes to explain, she would at least have some answers. He'd asked for time to pray and sort things through. She wanted to honor that, but wasn't five days long enough?

What would Wes say if he knew about Toby's problems and Mrs. Barlow's recommendation? Tilley loved them, but she hadn't been feeling well all week, and Lauren didn't want to add to her burdens. Julia was away in Burlington for a real estate conference and wouldn't return until late Sunday. She really didn't have any other close friends in Tipton…except Wes.

She glanced at the phone, debating her choices. It was early afternoon. Wes was probably still working at the Nature Center. What if she and Toby took a drive over to Wild River? Would Wes welcome their visit? Or would that only make things more difficult for everyone?

Chapter Fourteen

Wes grinned and poked Bill in the ribs. "Look up there." He pointed to the open rafters above the Nature Center auditorium, where a large barn owl had roosted in the corner. The owl blinked and quietly scanned the crowd below. He had an unusual heart-shaped face and large, wise-looking eyes.

"Don't worry," Bill said. "Chet knows the owl's up there. The same thing happened last year when he did this program. You watch. He'll call the bird down in a few minutes."

Chet Davis, a visiting naturalist with a program on birds of prey, stood in front of the auditorium speaking to a group of about sixty homeschooled children and their parents. A few younger children wiggled on the wooden benches, but the rest stared with rapt attention as the speaker introduced his next feathered friend.

Wes crossed his arms and leaned against the back

wall. This guy was amazing. He not only entertained the kids, he taught them more about birds of prey than they'd ever learn from a book. So far he'd shown them a red-tailed hawk, two peregrine falcons and a tiny northern pygmy owl—and he was only about fifteen minutes into his forty-minute presentation.

Bill nudged him. "Hey, look who's here."

Wes followed Bill's gaze and his heart jerked in his chest. Lauren stood in the auditorium doorway, holding Toby's hand. She looked intently around the room as though she was searching for someone. Her gaze connected with his and held.

He smiled and a look of relief washed over her face.

Toby's eyes lit up when he spotted Wes. He dropped his mother's hand and made a beeline for Wes.

Wes squatted down to greet him, and Toby rewarded him with a tight hug. He held the boy for a moment, touched by the emotion conveyed in his embrace, and then leaned back to look into his face. "How are you doing, buddy?"

"I'm okay." Toby's gap-toothed grin spread wider. His nose glowed bright pink from the cold weather, and his blond hair stood out with static. Wes guessed he had just pulled off the red knit hat in his hand.

"Hello, Wes." Lauren's soft greeting vibrated through him. He stood to face her. She smiled hesitantly, looking as beautiful as ever, and he could barely resist the urge to pull her in for a hug as Toby had done with him.

"Hi." He smiled, feeling foolishly tongue-tied and so happy to see them he could barely hold it in.

"Looks like you're busy." Her smile faded as she glanced around the full room and at the program in progress.

"No, not really. I'm just here for crowd control. But there's no problem with this group."

Her gaze traveled back to meet his. "Could we talk for a few minutes? I need some advice."

Urgency pulsed through him. She wanted to talk. He definitely wanted to listen. Wes turned to Bill. "Can I take a break?"

"Sure. No problem. How about I take Toby up front so he can see the program?" He placed his hand on Toby's shoulder. "I think Chet's going to bring out the eagles next. You don't want to miss that."

Toby looked up at Lauren, his eyes glowing with excitement. "Can I go see them, Mom?"

She hesitated, looking uncertain.

Bill smiled reassuringly. "It's okay. I'll keep an eye on him. You two go ahead."

Lauren bent down and looked into Toby's eyes. "You stay with Bill and be a good listener, okay?"

Toby grinned and nodded. Bill took his hand and led him through the crowd to the front, where he squeezed Toby in on the first-row bench.

Wes studied Lauren as she watched her son to be sure he was safely settled. Concern clouded her eyes. Something was obviously troubling her.

"Let's go to the office. It's quiet back there."

"Okay," she said softly.

He resisted the urge to reach for her arm or take her hand as he moved toward Bill's office. He didn't want to rush ahead and scare her off or send the wrong message.

A ripple of apprehension traveled through him as he wondered what had prompted her visit. He blew out a slow breath and shook off his concern. Whatever the reason, he was glad she'd come. Seeing her again was an answer to his prayers. She was seeking him out and wanted his help and advice.

He could see it in her eyes. Lauren was opening the door again. Now if he only had the courage to walk through it and be the man she needed.

Lauren settled into the chair opposite Bill's desk and unbuttoned her coat. Wes had offered to get her a cup of coffee and she'd gratefully agreed. She needed a moment to settle her heart and prepare her words just as much as she needed a caffeine boost. The nervousness she'd felt on her drive over had faded a little when she'd seen Wes's warm smile, but now she'd have to tell him why she'd come. What would he think about her coming to talk to him about Toby's problems?

She glanced around the cluttered office. Three shelves full of nature books covered the wall behind the desk, and an interesting collection of birds was displayed in a glass case beside her. A stuffed raccoon with a black mask and ringed tail stood poised on the top of the filing cabinet, and a large moose head, complete with massive, pronged antlers, hung on the wall above the door. She smiled. This was definitely a man's office.

Wes walked in carrying two steaming mugs of coffee. He passed her one and took a seat in the brown leather chair behind the desk.

"So, what's up?" He leaned back in his chair and took a sip from his mug. He looked interested but relaxed and comfortable with her being there.

That sent a surge of confidence through her. It hadn't been a mistake to come. This was the right thing to do.

"Toby's having a rough time at school. His teacher called twice this week, and now she's pushing to have him evaluated by special services."

Lauren poured out her concern for Toby. She even touched on her worst fear: that his failures at school might permanently damage his life. Wes listened quietly, giving her his full attention. Finally, she ran out of words and sat back. He probably thought she was an overprotective, neurotic mother who couldn't see past the end of her nose where her son was concerned.

"So what are you going to do?" he asked.

"I'm not sure. I was hoping you might have some wisdom for me."

His mouth quirked in a small smile. "Well, I don't have much experience with situations like this."

"I know, but you seem to connect with Toby." She leaned forward and placed her hands on the desk. "You see past the surface with people. You care."

He rubbed his chin and seemed to ponder her words for a moment. Then he focused on her. "His teacher wants this evaluation and you don't, right?"

"I'm not sure, but I definitely don't want him labeled or classified."

"Maybe you could meet with the school counselor or the principal. Share your concerns with them and find out more about the evaluation. Then you'll have more information to make the best decision for Toby."

"I do want what's best for him."

"Of course you do, but don't let them talk you into something you're not comfortable with just because they have a degree or a title. You know Toby better than anyone else, and you have more at stake. You love him." Wes smiled. "Don't worry. You'll make the right decision."

"Thanks, Wes." His words warmed her heart. It felt so good to hear someone express confidence in her ability to make the right choices for her son. She loved Toby more than her own life, and seeing him grow up happy and healthy was more important to her than opening her gallery or anything else.

He set his coffee mug on the desk, leaned forward and clasped his hands. "Here's another idea that might help. When I was in college, I got involved in the Big Brothers program. I met with a boy named Zach a couple of times a week for over two years. We really hit it off. Maybe I could do that same kind of thing with Toby."

"I know he'd love it…but I don't see the connection with his schoolwork."

"Toby is probably discouraged because he's having such a hard time. But if I spent time with him, he could try some sports or get involved in things here at the Nature Center. Maybe that would help him develop other interests and build his confidence so he could cope with the challenges at school."

Gratefulness flooded her heart as she listened to his suggestion. "That would be great."

"And if you don't get the help and answers you want from his school, maybe you could teach him yourself."

"You mean homeschool him?"

"Yes. I was talking to a few of the parents who came for the program today. It sounds like they have a good network of families in this area. Maybe homeschooling would take the pressure off. He wouldn't have to compete or compare himself to everyone else. He could just move ahead at his own pace."

Lauren drew in a slow breath, turning over the idea in her mind. "I've never really thought about homeschooling before."

"I've heard some good things about it. And after watching the behavior of the group that's out there now compared to the school groups we've had in here this week, I think homeschooling must have some definite merit."

Lauren smiled. Could she homeschool her son? She already spent an hour or two almost every evening helping Toby with reading and homework in just about every subject. On those days he missed school, she often did the whole day's assignments in that much time. How much harder could it be?

She glanced back at Wes. "I'll look into it and see what's involved."

He smiled and nodded. "Good." His gaze remained fixed on her, and she had a feeling he was pleased with more than just her response to his suggestions for Toby.

Wes slipped his hands in his jeans pockets as he stood at the front window of the Nature Center and watched Lauren and Toby drive off. He sighed and turned away, wishing he was leaving with them. That one short hour together hardly seemed like enough. But he had the promise of seeing her tomorrow. Bill had given him Saturday off, and Wes had offered to spend part of the afternoon with Toby. In fact, he'd convinced Lauren to let him see Toby on Tuesday and Thursday after school, as well. Would he be able to spend time with Lauren, too? He smiled at the possibility and shot off a quick prayer, asking for wisdom.

"Hey, Wes, would you run these time sheets up to the front office?" Bill walked toward him with the papers in one hand and a broom in the other. "That is, unless you'd rather sweep up." Bill lifted his dark brows and grinned. Feathers, candy wrappers and a few bird droppings remained on the floor from the day's program.

"You sure you want to give me that choice?"

Bill nodded. "Have you met Nancy the bookkeeper?"

"No, why?"

"That woman gives the word flirt new meaning. She definitely doesn't know how to take no for an answer. I'd prefer sweeping bird droppings any day."

Wes chuckled. "Don't worry. I'll take care of it." He held out his hand for the time sheets.

"Thanks." Bill set to work sweeping.

Wes grabbed his coat from a hook on the back of Bill's office door. He left the Nature Center and crossed the parking lot to the main lodge. Wes passed the café, noting the tantalizing aromas of french fries and hot dogs.

He turned down the hall leading to the resort offices, and Ryan Zeller stepped out of his father's door. Recognition flashed in Ryan's eyes when he saw Wes. Rather than moving aside, he turned to face Wes, blocking his path.

"What are you doing here?" Ryan crossed his arms and looked Wes over with a scornful glance.

Wes smiled slightly. He towered over Ryan, and it struck him as funny that the smaller man intentionally stood in his way. Did he think his family's ownership of Wild River gave him the right to treat everyone with contempt?

"I work in the Nature Center."

Surprise flickered in Ryan's eyes, but he quickly masked it. "Is that right? Since when?"

"Since your father hired me last week."

Ryan snorted and shook his head. "Wow, I knew we were hard up for help, but I had no idea we were scraping the bottom of the barrel."

Anger flashed through Wes, but he held on

to his temper. "Excuse me." He moved to step around Ryan.

Ryan thrust out his arm. "Where do you think you're going?"

Wes halted, straining to keep himself in check, but the memory of Ryan's rude encounters with Lauren stoked the fire of his anger. "What's your problem?"

"I don't have a problem. You do. If you want to keep your job, you better stay away from Lauren Woodman."

Indignation burned Wes's throat and he glared at Ryan. "Are you threatening me?"

Ryan scowled, his blue-gray eyes darkening like storm clouds. "No, I'm giving you a warning. My family owns Wild River. If I say the word, you're fired."

"Your father hired me. If he has a problem with the way I do my job, he can talk to me." Wes pushed past, knocking Ryan's arm out of the way.

"I mean it, Evans. Stay away from her." Ryan's angry voice reverberated off the walls.

Wes strode away and shoved open the door at the end of the hall. Stepping outside, he pulled in a deep breath of cold air and blew it out slowly, waiting for his heartbeat to slow down. Ryan Zeller obviously didn't want him involved with Lauren, but why was he so hostile about it?

He closed his eyes, remembering the time Ryan had interrupted their dinner at the potluck. His cocky attitude and suggestive remarks had angered Wes and upset Lauren. What had Lauren said about him? *We went to school together…his family owns Wild River.* Nothing significant. There'd been no indication she liked him. In fact, the opposite seemed true. But they must share some kind of history.

What was their connection?

Chapter Fifteen

"Look, there's Wild River." Wes pointed across the wooded valley to the lodge and ski slopes on the far side. Even at a distance, he could see skiers and snowboarders dotting the hillsides and riding the chairlifts.

"Pick me up. I wanna see." Toby held up his arms and Wes lifted the boy onto his shoulders. Laughing, Toby placed his cold, wet gloves over Wes's eyes.

"Oh no, now I'm blind." Wes grabbed Toby's legs and staggered around, giving him a wild ride and good reason to hold on tighter.

Toby giggled. "You're not blind." He pulled his little hands away and leaned down to look into Wes's face. "Turn around. I want to see Wild River."

"Okay." Wes tramped through the snow to a break in the trees where Toby would have a better view. "There's the lodge, and next to that is the Nature Center, where you watched the bird program last week." Wes pointed out the buildings to Toby. "And if you follow that road past the Nature Center and go over the bridge, you'll see my place."

"Your house?"

"Yes, that's where I live with Bill."

"I want to go to your house." The boy rocked back and forth as though he were riding Wes like a horse.

"That sounds fun, but not today." They'd spent the last hour behind Toby's school, flying down the best sledding hill in Tipton.

"Couldn't we *please* go to your house?"

"Sorry, buddy. We made a deal with your mom, remember? We have to be back before dinner, and you have to do your homework with a good attitude tonight."

Toby groaned. "I don't wanna do any more schoolwork."

Wes patted the boy's leg, remembering the struggle he faced at school. Lauren said his attitude had been a little better this week—at least there had been no more stomachaches or crying to stay home. "I know homework isn't fun. But it's important, and we need to keep our promise to your mom. How about you come over to my house on Saturday?"

"No, not Saturday. That's my mom's birthday."

Wes lifted Toby off his shoulders and set him on the ground. He squatted in front of the boy, searching his face. "Are you sure that's her birthday?"

Toby nodded with wide-eyed sincerity. "Yep. Aunt Tilley took me to the store and we bought her a present. But I can't tell you what it is 'cause it's a secret."

Wes smiled and squeezed Toby's shoulder. "That's okay. You've already told me what I need to know." Lauren's birthday was only two days away, and that gave him just enough time to do something about it.

Lauren hooked her arm through Julia's as they walked toward the back door at Long Meadow. Moonlight lit the neatly shoveled path. She smiled, remembering how Wes had insisted on clearing away the snow when he'd dropped Toby off on Thursday after sledding.

Her thoughts of Wes were bittersweet. He had faithfully spent time with Toby every Tuesday, Thursday and Saturday for the past two weeks, but he'd only greeted her in passing. He hadn't given a hint that he remembered the kiss they'd shared. He was kind and caring, but there seemed to be an invisible line he would not cross. At first she'd been relieved. Then she'd been bothered.

She sighed, and let it go. Today was her birthday, and she wouldn't let anything spoil it—not even disappointment over her *almost* romance with Wes.

"Thanks for suggesting a movie," Lauren said. "That was fun."

"I'm glad you liked it." Julia plunged her hands in her pockets.

"Can you stay for dinner?" Lauren stepped onto the back porch. "Tilley's been cooking since this morning. She wouldn't even let me in the kitchen to fix myself lunch."

Julia laughed. "Well, I'm sure she wanted to

make you something special for tonight. And yes, I'd love to stay."

Lauren nodded and smiled as she pushed open the back door. The tantalizing aroma of Mexican food greeted her as she stepped inside, making her mouth water. She hung up her coat, listening for voices, but she didn't hear anyone—not even the dog.

Walking into the dimly lit kitchen, she glanced around. A ripple of apprehension traveled up her back. The table had not been set, and the only light came from two candles flickering on the open shelves of the buffet.

"That's funny. I wonder where they went." She glanced at Julia.

Her friend shrugged and smiled.

"Surprise!" a chorus of voices shouted behind her, and the lights flashed on.

Lauren gasped and spun around. Six jubilant faces filled the entryway leading into the dining room, but her gaze fastened on Wes, standing tall behind her son.

Laughing, Julia gave her a quick hug. "We gotcha!"

Happily stunned, Lauren's gaze traveled around the group. Pastor Dan Shelton put his arm around his wife, Marie, and smiled at Lauren. Bill grinned and waved. Tilley stood next to him, her old blue eyes twinkling.

Toby clapped his hands and jumped up and down. "We surprised her! We surprised her!"

Joy bubbled from her laughter as she crossed the

room and hugged her son. "You sure did! So…you planned this party for me?"

He nodded vigorously. "Yep. Me and Wes. We did it."

Lauren's heartbeat quickened at that news. "I wondered what you two were laughing about this morning. I should have figured it out." She kissed her son's cheek and looked up at Wes.

He placed his hands on Toby's shoulders. "Happy birthday, Lauren." The affection in his eyes and smile echoed in his voice.

Her heart felt as soft as warm wax. "Thank you, Wes. I haven't had a birthday party in a long time."

Tilley leaned over and gave her a quick kiss on the cheek. "Well, you deserve a special celebration. I made your favorite—chicken enchiladas. Come on everyone. Let's sit down."

Tilley ushered everyone into the dining room amid more laughter and good wishes. Lauren's heart lifted when she saw the pink-and-white streamers hung from corner to corner and a cluster of pink helium balloons tied to the chair at the end of the table. Tilley had set out her best rose-patterned china and crystal water glasses. Fresh flowers and candles added a festive touch to the table.

"Oh, this is beautiful. Thank you."

Wes caught her hand and led her to the head of the table. His warm grasp sent a message that made her heart do a funny little flip-flop. "You can have a seat right here." He pulled out her chair and then lifted his brows and motioned to Toby.

Her son reached under the table and pulled out a

crown made of pink construction paper and generously sprinkled with silver glitter. "I made this for you. Just like we get at school on our birthday." He held the crown out for her to see, obviously very proud of his creation.

Lauren smiled as she read the number twenty-eight printed on the front. "It's beautiful."

Standing on tiptoe, Toby placed the crown on her head.

"I feel so special. Thank you, sweetie." She kissed her son's cheek, her heart overflowing with love for him.

Everyone else took a seat, and Tilley asked Wes to say the blessing. Lauren bowed her head and, just before she closed her eyes, Wes laid his hand over hers.

"Father, thank You for Lauren. And thank You for blessing each one of us by our friendship with her. We're grateful we can honor her tonight and celebrate her special day. Thank You for all You've done in her life this past year. Please meet every need for her and pour out Your very best blessings on her in this next year. We ask You to be our special guest at the table tonight as we celebrate and enjoy the evening together. In Jesus' name, amen."

Emotion clogged her throat as she listened to Wes's prayer and felt the warmth of his hand on hers. She didn't deserve any of this. It didn't make sense. Of course she and Julia were close, but she hardly knew Pastor Dan or his wife Marie, and she'd only met Bill a few months ago at church. She swallowed and blinked away her tears.

As soon as the prayer was finished, Wes slipped

his hand away, but he leaned closer and whispered, "I hope you don't mind having your age on the crown. Toby really wanted to write it, and I thought it was a good project for him."

Lauren smiled and lifted her hand to adjust the paper crown. "I don't mind at all. In fact, I'm very proud I made it all the way to twenty-eight."

His gaze grew tender. "So am I," he said softly, so only she could hear.

Heat flushed her cheeks, but she didn't look away. Instead, she smiled at Wes and hoped her eyes would convey the feelings in her heart.

The laughter and lively conversation continued for well over an hour while they all enjoyed Tilley's delicious chicken enchiladas, Spanish rice, green beans almandine and spinach-orange salad. Toby grew a little restless, but everyone made an effort to include him, and he only asked twice if it was time to bring in the cake.

Finally, Tilley patted his hand. "All right. Let's move into the living room to have dessert."

Toby scooted back from the table and hurried into the next room. He took a seat on one end of the couch near the fireplace. Lauren sat next to him and patted his leg. Wes followed and took a seat on the other side of Lauren. A warm glow of pleasure filled her as he settled in and slipped his arm across the back of the couch behind her.

Tilley peeked her head in the living room. "Toby, I could use your help in the kitchen." Her smile and quick wink seemed to send him a private message.

"Okay." He leaped from the couch wearing a big grin.

"Let me help, too," Marie offered and followed Toby toward the kitchen.

Wes leaned closer and smiled. "He's been begging to light the candles all afternoon."

The doorbell chimed and Lauren looked at Wes. "Are we expecting more guests?"

He frowned slightly. "Not that I know of."

"Okay. I'll just see who it is." She got up and crossed to the front door, an odd sensation traveling through her. Most of their friends came to the back door. She flipped on the porch light, pulled open the door and sucked in a startled gasp.

Ryan Zeller tilted his head and grinned. "Hi, Lauren."

"What are you doing here?" she whispered, then darted a glance over her shoulder.

He laughed, but at least he had the decency to look uncomfortable. "Come on, Lauren. That's not a very nice greeting."

She narrowed her eyes, trying to make sense of his unannounced visit. Did he expect her to invite him in? There was no way she wanted him in her house or anywhere near her son.

He shrugged and grew more serious. "I heard it was your birthday." He reached into his jacket and pulled out a white envelope. "I came to give you this."

"Why…why would you give me anything?"

He pressed his lips together and then looked down at his feet. "Because I know I upset you before and I want to apologize."

His sincere expression shook her. Was he truly sorry, or playing some kind of game?

He smiled again. "Now, can I please come in? It's freezing out here."

Lauren glanced over her shoulder once more. She couldn't see Wes from this angle. What would he think of Ryan's unexpected visit? But more importantly, what would Ryan say when he saw Toby again? Would he make the connection to his brother this time? Was that really why he'd come—to take another look at her son?

"Get ready to sing," Tilley called from the kitchen.

Lauren gripped the door handle, feeling trapped. If she didn't invite Ryan in, Tilley would. There was no way her aunt would allow a guest to be turned away from a party in progress. "All right. You can come in."

Lauren turned and walked back into the living room, wishing she could disappear and make this party vanish with her. She heard Ryan's footsteps cross the hardwood floor behind her and a sickening wave of nausea rose and burned her throat. She knew the moment Wes caught sight of Ryan. Surprise flashed in his eyes. He shot her a concerned look.

Lauren averted her gaze and took her seat next to Wes. Leaning forward, she clasped her hands near her knees, feeling as cold and rigid as an icicle. Ryan sat in the overstuffed chair facing her on the other side of the coffee table.

Wonderful! Now she would have to look at him for the rest of the evening.

"Happy birthday to you…" Tilley's sweet soprano voice rang out as she entered the room carrying Lauren's blazing birthday cake. Everyone joined in the song. Toby beamed as he carried in the dessert plates, walking beside Tilley. They set the cake on the coffee table in front of Lauren.

"Make a wish!" Toby leaned closer and pulled in a deep breath, preparing to help her blow out the candles.

She forced a smile for his sake, but she knew it would take much more than a birthday wish to straighten out this mess.

She closed her eyes and prayed. *Lord, help me make it through this party without hurting my son. I know he needs to hear the truth about his father someday, but I don't want to explain it to him tonight, not in front of everyone.*

Dread knotted her stomach. She opened her eyes and blew out the candles. Everyone clapped and cheered. She glanced around the circle of smiling faces. Even though they all seemed to be her friends, if they knew about the night of Toby's conception, they would turn their backs in disgust.

When the truth came out, and she had no doubt it eventually would, no one would want to have anything to do with her—not even Wes.

Chapter Sixteen

Lauren pulled the red plaid blanket more snugly around her shoulders and scooted the chair closer to the fireplace. Flames leaped from the glowing logs, sending radiant waves of warmth to her face. At least the part of her facing the fire was warm. She glanced at her watch and let loose a deep sigh. Leaning back, she closed her eyes.

How long could it take the repairman to drive out from West Harmon? It had been over four hours since she'd called Atlas Heating and Cooling, asking them to send a repairman to fix her broken furnace.

Opening her eyes, she stared into the flickering flames, contemplating the events of her party the previous night. How could an evening that had started out so magically change into such a nightmare?

When she'd opened the card from Ryan, a pair of season passes to Wild River fell out and landed on the coffee table. Ryan smiled and proudly announced his gift included private ski lessons for her and Toby—with him as the instructor. She stared at him, stunned and speechless. Her stomach swirled and she almost lost the birthday cake she had forced down for Toby's sake.

She wanted to scoop up the passes and shove them back at him. But how could she with everyone gathered around, smiling and complimenting Ryan for his generosity and thoughtfulness? To them, he looked like an old friend who remembered her birthday and just wanted to do something nice for her and her son.

But she knew the truth. There had never been a genuine friendship between them, and his appearance at her door was a frightening mystery she didn't want to solve.

Lauren had slipped the passes back in the envelope and laid it on the large book featuring colonial antiques she had just received from Julia. Then Tilley handed Lauren her next gift. She hurried to open it, hoping to take everyone's focus off Ryan and the passes.

When she pulled the lid off the gift box, she discovered a lovely turquoise scarf and hat knit by her aunt. Lauren tossed the scarf around her neck and pulled on the hat. Everyone applauded as she modeled Tilley's handiwork. Leaning down, she planted a kiss on Tilley's cheek and whispered her thanks.

Returning to the couch, she carefully folded the hat and scarf and laid them on the coffee table. Wes leaned closer and passed her a little square package wrapped in silver paper and tied with a pink satin ribbon. His smile had warmed her heart and made everyone else seem to fade out of focus. She slipped off the paper, opened the box and gasped at the exquisite gold cross necklace inside. "Oh, Wes, this is beautiful."

"Try it on," Julia had insisted.

Lauren smiled. Taking the necklace from the box, she held it out to Wes. "Will you help me hook it in the back?"

He had nodded and gently slipped the delicate gold chain around her neck. She lifted her hair out of the way so he could see the clasp. Then she turned and looked into his eyes. His smile deepened as his gaze rested on her, full of affection and approval. How she had wished they were alone so they could share what was in their hearts.

A log popped and sent a spark flying onto the hearth, stirring Lauren from her memories of the party. She lifted her hand and traced the outline of the cross pendant, remembering again Wes's tender glances and caring actions.

Sighing, she let her hand slip away. It was useless to dream about a deeper relationship with Wes.

This was the reality of her life: she had a freezing house, a half-finished gallery, a son with serious struggles at school and a shameful past that Ryan Zeller seemed ready to bring to light. How could she even think of romance? Especially when the only man she wanted to share it with was so much more spiritually committed than she would ever be.

If he really knew what she was like, he wouldn't want her.

The phone rang and she snatched it off the end table, hoping it was the repairman confirming the directions to Long Meadow. Instead, Julia greeted her and asked why she'd missed church. Lauren explained the broken furnace and the long wait for the repairman.

"Do you want me to bring you some hot soup?"

"No, Tilley left some chili in the Crock-Pot. I'll be fine." Lauren really hadn't felt like eating this morning with all the confusing thoughts of the party still spinning through her mind and tossing her stomach. But as the hours slipped by and her fears began to subside, the simmering chili smelled more enticing.

"So have you recovered from last night?" Julia asked.

"Not quite."

Julia laughed. "I wish I'd had my camera when they yelled 'Surprise.' You should have seen your face."

"Thanks. I'm sure I looked lovely with my mouth hanging open like that."

"Simply gorgeous. And I'm not the only one who thought so," Julia said in a teasing tone. "I hope you realize Wes was the mastermind behind the party. He planned everything except the food. Tilley wouldn't let him help with that." Julia's voice sounded dreamy. "That's one very special guy. I hope you're planning to hold on to him."

Lauren's heart surged with Julia's words, but she

quickly clamped a lid on those emotions. "Stop. I told you we're just friends."

"Well, you'd never know it from the way he was looking at you last night."

Lauren fiddled with the fringe on the blanket, secretly wishing it was true. "Julia, you have an imagination that doesn't quit."

"Hey, I'm not imagining anything. Didn't you see how he reacted when Ryan gave you those season passes?"

"What do you mean?" Lauren had been so focused on hiding her anxiety over Ryan's arrival she hadn't noticed Wes's response when she'd opened Ryan's card.

"His eyes were just about shooting daggers."

"Come on, you're making that up."

"No, I'm not! He had that stay-away-from-my-girl kind of look in his eyes."

"Really?" Lauren smiled in spite of the warning she gave herself.

"Yes! I can't believe you didn't notice." Julia paused for a moment. "You know what I don't get? How did Ryan know it was your birthday? Is there something going on between you two?"

"No!" Guilt coursed through Lauren, but she stuffed it deeper. "I have no idea how he found out about my birthday. I certainly didn't invite him over."

Lauren could almost picture Julia's puzzled expression. They had been friends since ninth grade but attended different colleges and only saw each other at Christmas break and in the summer during their college years. Lauren had never confessed the truth about her spring-vacation romance with Stephen Zeller.

"Maybe Bill told him about the party," Julia said.

Lauren released a slow breath. "Yes, that's probably how he heard about it."

Julia laughed softly. "Remember how you had such a huge crush on his brother, Stephen, when we were in school?"

Lauren's heart twisted and she squeezed her eyes closed. She wasn't ready to tell Julia or anyone the results of her foolish crush on Stephen Zeller. "That was a long time ago," she whispered in a choked voice.

"Isn't it awful what happened to Stephen? It doesn't seem right for someone so young to die like that. He'd skied all his life. Then he hit that tree and it was all over."

Lauren clutched the blanket to her throat. She didn't want to discuss Stephen's death. How could she explain the strange mixture of emotions she experienced every time she thought of his accident? The tug-of-war between relief and sorrow, vindication and guilt that jerked her emotions all over the place, leaving her confused and unsettled.

"Sorry. I probably shouldn't be talking about that."

Lauren heard a car pull into the gravel driveway. "I have to go. I think the repairman's here."

"Okay. I'll talk to you soon."

Lauren hung up the phone just as a knock sounded at the back door. Dropping the blanket from her shoulders, she headed to answer it and whispered a hurried prayer. *Lord, please help him fix it right away, and if it's not too much trouble, could You keep the cost down?*

Wes shot off a prayer as he stood on Lauren's back porch, waiting for her to answer the door. *Lord, help me get this right.* He juggled a toolbox in one hand and an electric space heater in the other. Hopefully, he could get her furnace going, warm up the house and find answers to the questions that had kept him awake half the night.

The door opened. Lauren looked out at him and blinked in surprise. She wore a baggy, dark green sweatshirt over a white turtleneck and her faded jeans had a hole in one knee, but she'd never looked better. Though it had only been about fourteen hours since he'd seen her last, it felt like forever.

"I heard you didn't have any heat." He lifted the toolbox in explanation. "Would you like me to take a look?"

She smiled and nodded. "Sure. Come in." The delight in her eyes sent hope spiraling through him.

Maybe he was worried about nothing. Then he remembered Ryan's unexpected arrival at the party last night. A choking cloud of doubt and frustration settled over him as the scene replayed in his mind.

When she'd opened Ryan's card and those two expensive season passes to Wild River fell out, jealousy and frustration had gripped Wes's heart. He'd barely been able to sit still. There was no way his little gift of a gold cross necklace could compare.

He'd spent a good part of last night wrestling and praying over the situation. Why would Ryan show up uninvited like that? Was he an old boyfriend who just wouldn't let Lauren go, or was it something else? His threats to Wes and Lauren's icy response to his arrival at the party pushed Wes's frustration level higher. What was going on between them? Not knowing was driving him to distraction. He'd hardly heard the sermon that morning. Instead, he'd sat in church wondering why Lauren hadn't come. He made up his mind after the service to visit her that afternoon. And he wasn't leaving until they settled things.

Lauren ushered him through the kitchen. "Thanks for coming over. I called a repairman, but he hasn't shown up yet." She slowed and glanced over her shoulder as she pushed open the basement door. "How did you hear about my broken furnace?"

He paused and set the heater down. "I was waiting for you at church. When you didn't come, I asked Tilley where you were." His confession made his neck and face burn. But that was okay. He didn't want to hide his interest any longer. She needed to know how he felt. And if he wanted her to be truthful about Ryan, he'd have to be honest about his own feelings.

She stopped on the top step and turned to him. "You were waiting for me?" Her eyes glimmered and a small smile lifted the corners of her mouth.

He nodded. "I always look for you." Suddenly, his tongue felt thick and stuck to the roof of his mouth.

Her lips parted. She scanned his face, waiting for him to say more.

He glanced into her eyes, debating his next words. Standing on the basement steps with a toolbox in his hand didn't seem like the right setting for this important conversation. Perhaps he'd better do the repair work and wait for another opportunity. He cleared his throat. "Why don't I take a look at your furnace and see if I can figure out what's going on?"

She tipped her head and smiled, looking a little puzzled. "Okay."

He fiddled with the furnace for about fifteen minutes, berating himself the entire time. If he couldn't work up the courage to tell her how he felt, then how did he expect her to share what was in her heart?

Lauren hung around watching him for a few minutes but then retreated to the kitchen to fix lunch. His frustration mounted as he realized he didn't have the slightest idea how to bring her dead furnace back to life. He'd worked on gas heaters and hot-water radiators, but never on an ancient oil furnace like this one. He dropped the wrench on his toe and it sent pain shooting through his foot. Biting back the words that came to mind, he bent to pick up the wrench, only to bang his head on a pipe as he stood.

Blowing out a disgusted breath, he rubbed the back of his head and squatted on the cold cement floor. His head throbbed and his shoulders drooped with frustration. Inadequacy flooded his soul. *Lord, I'm struggling here. And I don't just mean with this broken-down old furnace. Could You please give me a hand?*

He waited in silence for an answer, but the only sound he heard was Lauren's soft footsteps coming down the stairs. "How's it going?"

He laid the wrench back in the toolbox and sent her an apologetic grin. "I hope you didn't cancel that repairman."

She slipped her hands in her back pockets and grinned. "Not yet."

"Good, 'cause you still need him." He shook his head. "Sorry, I was hoping I could save you some money."

"It's okay. I appreciate you trying. How about some lunch?"

He nodded, picked up the toolbox and followed her upstairs, his spirits lifting a little. Within five minutes they were seated on the couch in the living room, facing the fire and holding bowls of Tilley's homemade chili. Wes's mouth watered as he took his first spoonful, topped with sour cream and cheddar cheese. A large plate of corn bread sat on the coffee table between them, and Wes knew it would be the perfect partner for the spicy chili. They ate in companionable silence for a few minutes, watching the fire and enjoying its warmth.

Wes turned to Lauren. "So, did we really surprise you last night?"

She laughed. "Yes. Couldn't you tell?" She made a silly shocked face that looked nothing like she had last night.

He'd never forget the way her eyes had sparkled

when he'd taken her hand and led her to the special chair at the head of the table.

"I thought you might just be acting surprised for Toby's sake."

"No. I had no idea." She wiped her mouth with a napkin and reached for a piece of corn bread. "Thanks for letting Toby help. It's good to see him learn how to give to others and find joy in that."

Wes smiled and nodded. Watching Toby make the paper crown and put up balloons and streamers had been almost as much fun as seeing Lauren's response. "Yeah, he was pretty excited. I wasn't sure if he'd be able to keep the secret."

"He did." Her soft laughter and gentle smile filled an empty place deep in his heart.

Wes reached over and set his bowl next to the pile of birthday presents on the coffee table. The envelope from Ryan lay on top of the book Julia had given Lauren. His stomach clenched. "Are you going to take Toby skiing with those passes?"

She shifted her gaze to the bowl in her lap. "I haven't been downhill skiing for years."

"You shouldn't let that stop you."

"I don't even know if I'd remember how."

"Well, you're great at cross-country skiing. It can't be much harder."

"It's a totally different sport. I was never good at downhill."

Wes huffed. "Sounds like Ryan would be more than happy to give you lessons as long as he's the teacher."

She shot him a confused glance.

He grimaced. "Sorry. Guess I'm feeling a little put out that he crashed your party and gave you those passes."

She set her half-eaten bowl of chili on the coffee table and took a sip of her water. The silence stretched uncomfortably between them.

He shifted and turned to face her. "Lauren, can I ask you a question?"

Her gaze darted back to him, apprehension flickering in her eyes. "What?"

"How did Ryan know it was your birthday?"

A coral glow spread across her cheeks, and she stared into the fire. "I'm not sure."

He waited, giving her time to explain. When she didn't, his irritation cranked up a notch. "Well, he must have some pretty strong feelings for you or he wouldn't give you such an expensive gift."

Her shoulders straightened. "Those passes didn't cost him anything. His family owns Wild River."

He shrugged, conceding her point. "Maybe, but I'd still say giving you that kind of gift makes a statement."

"What do you mean?" She set her napkin and corn bread on the table and turned to him, the challenge evident in her eyes.

"Lauren, those passes are worth over eight hundred dollars, whether he paid for them or not. Someone who's just an old friend wouldn't give you a big gift like that."

"So what do you want me to say?"

"I'd like you to tell me what's going on."

She lifted her hands, looking exasperated. "I have

no idea. I haven't talked to Ryan since the community potluck. I didn't tell him it was my birthday, and I didn't invite him over here."

"Maybe he remembered from before."

"What do you mean, 'before'?" Her eyes flashed a warning.

"Come on, Lauren. Why are you playing games? You two must have some kind of history together or he wouldn't just show up on your birthday and want to take you skiing."

Her face blanched and her expression hardened. "Why are you asking me all these questions?"

"I think you owe me an explanation."

"Why? Just because you throw me a birthday party and spend some time with my son doesn't mean I have to tell you about every relationship I've ever had."

Her words pierced him like a knife. He stared at her for several painful seconds. "You're right. You don't owe me anything."

He tossed his wadded napkin on the table and stalked toward the front door. Grabbing his coat from the bench, he shoved his arms in the sleeves and strode outside. Without a backward glance, he climbed into Bill's truck and roared down the driveway.

Chapter Seventeen

Wes blew dust off the top of the old file box and lifted the lid. "What did you say we're looking for?"

Bill shook his head and grinned. "You didn't hear a word I just said, did you?"

"Sorry." Wes knew he should have been listening, but his stormy conversation with Lauren kept replaying through his mind, distracting him. Though two days had passed, he couldn't get it out of his thoughts. He'd let his emotions take the lead, and he'd made a fool of himself. But worse than that, he'd broken the bridge of trust he'd worked so hard to build between them.

Bill slapped him on the back and sent him an understanding look. He knew what was going on. Wes had spilled the whole story as soon as he'd returned home from Lauren's on Sunday afternoon.

"Mr. Zeller wants us to set up a display, sort of a pictorial history of Wild River for the resort's twentieth anniversary."

Wes nodded and forced himself to put aside thoughts of Lauren as he began sorting through the file box. "So you want to show how Wild River looked then compared to now?"

"I'm not sure. Let's see what we've got to work with."

"Hey, here's an interesting one." Wes pulled a photo from the box. "Take a look at this." He held out a picture of the opening-day ribbon-cutting ceremony. A much younger Arthur Zeller stood in front of the doors to the main lodge, scissors in hand, ready to clip the red ribbon and open the resort.

Bill leaned closer. "Wow, Mr. Zeller used to have hair."

Wes chuckled. "Yeah, it looks like it." He set that photo aside and sorted through several others. Then his gaze fell on another photo of Arthur Zeller, smiling proudly and dressed in a ski jacket and knit hat. Two young boys stood with him, one on each side. Zeller rested his hands on the boys' shoulders. Wes glanced at the back, but he found no names or dates written there.

He turned it over and scanned the boys' faces, then squinted and looked closer. The boy on the left with the toothless grin looked amazingly familiar. Recognition jolted through Wes. He pulled in a sharp breath and his stomach spiraled toward his feet.

The resemblance was unmistakable. Father, son... and grandson. Stunned, Wes stared at the photo and tried to think of another explanation. Pain and anger twisted into a tight fist and leveled a blow at his heart.

"Find something interesting?" Bill asked.

Wes gripped the photo, fighting the urge to shred it to pieces. If only he could pretend he'd never seen it. But he had.

"Who's this?" He held the photo out to Bill with an unsteady hand, praying his friend would tell him he was imagining things.

Bill took the photo and studied the image. After a second he shot a quick glance back at Wes. "That's Art Zeller, and those are probably his sons, Ryan and Stephen."

"Look at the boy on the left. Who does he remind you of?"

Bill frowned and examined the photo once more. Slowly, his expression changed. Apprehension rippled across his face. He lifted his gaze to meet Wes's. Sympathy flashed in his eyes, and he quickly glanced away. "I'm not sure."

"Come on, Bill. Tell me what you think."

"Well…" His friend frowned and scanned the photo again. "He looks sort of like Toby."

Wes pressed his lips together and nodded. "That's what I thought." Lauren had lied to him. Closing his eyes, he fought the storm rising in his chest. "No wonder Ryan doesn't want me anywhere near Lauren. He's Toby's father."

"Hey, you don't know that for sure." Bill laid the photo on the desk and sent him an uneasy glance.

"What other explanation could there be?" Wes

stared at the photo. The boy smiled back at him with a carefree grin, and pain sliced straight through his heart.

Lauren dipped her paintbrush into the creamy butter-yellow paint and wiped off the extra on the inside edge of the can. She climbed one step higher on the ladder and applied her brush to the wall by the front window of her barn-turned-gallery.

Her empty stomach complained, reminding her she had long since worked off her lunch. She glanced at her watch and decided to keep going. Toby would be home in about forty-five minutes. She would take a break then and have a snack with him before Wes arrived…*if* Wes arrived.

He hadn't called to confirm his time with Toby as he usually did, and Lauren suspected he was still angry with her. She sighed and wearily shook her head. She was not going to waste any more time or energy trying to analyze the situation or sort out her feelings. What was the use? She had no future with Wes. Too much separated them. She needed to accept that and let it go, no matter how much it hurt.

But what if he didn't come today? What would she tell Toby? He had been doing so much better since he'd been spending time with Wes.

She heard gravel crunch on the driveway as a car pulled to a stop in back of the house. Glancing outside, she spotted Wes climbing out of Bill's truck and almost dropped her paintbrush.

He closed the door and walked toward the back porch.

Good! Let Tilley deal with him. She frowned and bit her lip as she watched him knock and wait for someone to answer. He didn't usually come until four o'clock. What was he doing here now? Had he come early to talk to her? She hadn't spoken to him since his inquisition Sunday afternoon. His probing questions and self-righteous attitude had pushed her too far.

She heard the screen door bang and glanced outside once more. Wes hustled down the steps and strode toward the barn, a frown creasing his forehead.

Apprehension rippled up her back. She climbed down the ladder on shaky legs and set aside her brush. Her stomach churned and her mind spun in crazy circles. *Oh, Lord, help!* She heard the knock, and the door opened before she could even respond.

Wes stood in the doorway, his expression calm and serious. "Can I come in?" As he waited on the doorstep, some undefined emotion flashed in his eyes. Then he looked away, drawing a curtain over his feelings.

She swallowed and nodded. He stepped inside and glanced around the interior of the barn. She stared at her speckled hands and grabbed an old rag to wipe them. Anything was preferable to looking into Wes's eyes.

"Lauren, we need to talk." His urgent tone surprised her.

She looked up and her heart melted at the poignant message now clearly written in his eyes.

She nodded and led the way to an old wooden

bench. He followed and took a seat next to her, close enough for her to feel the warmth of him right through her old paint-spattered jeans and sweatshirt.

He leaned forward and clasped his hands, quiet and serious. She watched his Adam's apple rise and fall above the neck of his brown sweater. "I'm sorry about Sunday. I never should've grilled you like that." He turned to her. "I hope you'll forgive me."

All her resentment washed away, and tears filled her eyes. "It's not your fault. I'm the one who was wrong. I'm pretty sure why Ryan came over...but I didn't want to tell you." Her throat grew thick and choked off her voice.

He leaned closer, his shoulder touching hers. "It's okay. You don't have to tell me. I know."

She turned and stared at him. "But how could you? I've never told anyone here, not even Tilley or Julia."

A sad smile touched his lips. "I was going through some old photos at Wild River." He pulled a photo from his jacket pocket and held it out to her. "I found this."

She took the picture and looked at the man and the two young boys. Recognition jolted through her and she began to tremble. The taller boy on the left had to be Stephen Zeller. His broad smile, shining eyes and upturned nose were almost a perfect reflection of Toby.

She swallowed hard and looked back at Wes. He watched her closely, but she saw no judgment or anger in his eyes, only sorrow and tenderness that urged her to speak.

"He's Toby's father," she whispered.

Wes nodded, silently waiting.

For so many years, she'd hidden the truth, tried to pretend it didn't matter. She'd hoped her silence would somehow erase the past and make it disappear. But she had a huge hole in her heart, a deep wound that had never healed. Now the person she had most wanted to hide it from had discovered the truth for himself.

"Tell me what happened," he said in a gentle voice as he reached for her hand and wrapped his big fingers around hers.

Anxiety rippled through her, raising goose bumps on her arms, but as she looked into Wes's eyes a glimmer of hope rose in her heart.

Wes rubbed his thumb over the top of her hand, praying she would finally tell him the story. Not so much because he needed to know, but because she needed to tell someone if she was ever going to release the pain she carried.

"I had a crush on him all through high school," she began slowly. "I don't think he even knew my name back then. He was fun and outgoing, and I was a total bookworm. He could have had just about any girl he wanted, and he definitely didn't want me."

Wes read the pain in her eyes. He wanted to tell her Ryan was an idiot for not noticing her, but he kept quiet and let her continue the story.

"We all went away to college, and when I came home on spring break my junior year I ran into him in town. I could hardly believe it when he stopped to talk to me." She hesitated and pushed her hair behind her shoulder. "I'd changed a lot. I got contacts and cut my hair, but I was still surprised when he asked me out. We went to a movie and had a good time, but he was…pretty aggressive." A flush crept up her neck and into her cheeks. "I should've seen what was coming."

Anger surged through Wes. Now he wished he'd flattened Ryan during their last confrontation at Wild River.

"He wanted to see me every day, and then on the Friday night before Easter, he invited me to a party at Wild River. The lodge was closed, but he had a key. I knew he hung out with a wild crowd, but he wanted me to come, and I so much wanted to believe that he really liked me."

Wes's stomach tensed as he watched her shake her head sadly. He pressed his lips together, determined to listen quietly without making any judgments or saying anything that would shut her down.

"Tilley didn't want me to go, but she said I was old enough to make up my own mind. So I went. It was worse than I'd expected. People were drinking and couples were all over each other. I wasn't a Christian then, but I knew it was wrong and I was in a dangerous situation. I thought having a boyfriend and being accepted by that group would give me what I needed to feel good about myself." She closed her eyes for a moment.

"I couldn't have been more wrong. As soon as we got there he brought me a drink. At first I said no, but he teased me and finally after we were dancing, I got thirsty and drank it. I'd never had any alcohol before, except champagne once at a wedding, so I didn't know how it would affect me. One drink didn't seem to do anything, so I thought two would be okay.

"But as soon as I took that second drink, I started to feel dizzy and sick. I finally told him I felt awful and wanted to go home. He just laughed and said I just needed to cool off and take a break. He took me to his father's office and we sat on the couch and talked, but then…I guess I passed out because I don't remember what happened after that."

She gripped his hand more tightly. "When I woke up the next morning, the couch had turned into a pullout bed, and I was laying there next to him under a rough old blanket." Her chin trembled. Tears flooded her eyes. She covered her face and began to sob.

He wrapped his arms around her and pulled her closer. She rested her head against his chest as she cried.

"Oh, Lauren, I'm so sorry," he whispered, closing his eyes, sharing her sorrow like it was his own.

Finally, her tears slowed and she sat up. But he kept his arm around her as she pulled a tissue from her pocket and blew her nose.

"All I wanted to do was get out of there, even if I had to walk home. I snuck out of the office and ran through the lodge, but the front door was locked and I couldn't get out. I felt so panicked and ashamed. I sank down right there by the front door and cried my eyes out. That's where Ryan found me. That's how he knows I spent the night with his brother."

A shock wave jolted through Wes. "Whoa, wait a minute. What do you mean, *his brother?*"

She looked at him strangely. Then she reached for the photo on the bench and pointed to the taller boy on the left. "This is Stephen, Ryan's older brother. He's the one I was talking about."

"Not Ryan?"

She shook her head.

Wes struggled to let go of his theory that Ryan was Toby's father and put this new information about Stephen in its place. "What happened to Stephen? Where is he?"

She looked up at him solemnly, tears washing her eyes again. "I never saw him again or even talked to him after that night." She pressed her lips together. "He died in a skiing accident about a year ago at Wild River. That's why I felt I could finally come back to Long Meadow."

Wes digested that information for a moment and then looked at Lauren again. "So Stephen and his family never knew about Toby?"

"No." She sniffed and wiped her eyes. "I never told anyone here in Tipton, but I think Ryan sees the resemblance and suspects Toby is Stephen's son."

Lauren's idea made sense, but Wes believed there was more going on with Ryan than she realized. He'd never told her about Ryan's warning to stay away from her. He considered mentioning it but decided not to. He wanted to focus on hearing the rest of Lauren's story. "So what happened after the party?"

"I went back to school and tried to pretend nothing was wrong, but I was a mess. I could hardly finish that semester. About two months later, I found out I was pregnant. I was too scared to come home for the summer or tell anyone, so I went to Boston with one of my college roommates and she took me in."

"You never told the police what happened?"

"How could I? I'd been drinking, and I didn't remember anything. Who'd believe me? The Zellers are the wealthiest and most influential family in this area. There's no way anyone could stand up against them with that kind of story."

"But what Stephen did was wrong. He should've gone to jail."

She shuddered and shook her head. "But I made the decision to go to that party. I accepted the drinks, even though I knew it was wrong. My own bad choices put me in that position. It's just as much my fault as Stephen's."

He gripped her hand, willing her to understand. "No one should take advantage of you like that. You were the victim, not a willing participant. And think about it, two drinks and you passed out? That doesn't make sense. He probably put something in your drink."

She looked at him skeptically. "I don't know."

Surprise rolled through him. Why couldn't she see it? Had she carried her guilt for so long that she couldn't even imagine that most of it actually belonged to someone else?

There was a path out of this valley of guilt. But

he doubted she was ready to hear that right now. It would take more than sharing a few Bible verses about forgiveness to heal her heart and restore what had been stolen. But he would show her what forgiveness looked like, and he would be there when she was ready to listen.

Chapter Eighteen

Wes whistled softly as he opened Bill's front door and stepped inside. Lauren's willingness to share the details of her past infused him with renewed hope for their relationship.

Wes glanced across the living room. Bill sat on the couch, reading the newspaper with his feet propped up on the coffee table. His friend lowered the paper and looked expectantly at him. "So, how did it go?"

Wes smiled. "Amazing."

"Really?"

"Yep. She explained everything."

"You're kidding." Bill folded the newspaper and laid it on the couch beside him. "What did she say?"

Wes pulled off his gloves and stuffed them in his jacket pockets. How much could he say without hurting Lauren? Bill had seen the photo and made assumptions about Ryan and Lauren that weren't true. At least he could straighten that out.

"Lauren should be the one to tell you the details, but I can tell you this much—Ryan isn't Toby's father."

Bill's eyes widened and he lowered his feet to the floor. "Wow, that boy looked so much like Toby. I thought for sure there was a connection between them."

Wes shrugged off his heavy jacket. "We were right about that. The boy in the picture *is* Toby's father…but it's not Ryan."

Bill's mouth dropped open. "It's Stephen?"

Frowning, Wes tossed his coat over the back of the brown leather chair. "Yeah, but don't say anything about this to anyone."

His friend's expression immediately grew more serious. "I won't."

Wes walked around the end of the couch and sat down. "Did you know Stephen?" He hoped Bill could tell him more about the man who had so drastically altered the course of Lauren's life.

Bill sat back. "I met him when I first started working at Wild River about four years ago. He was a good-looking guy but kind of overconfident and cocky. He made sure everyone knew his family owned the resort."

Wes nodded. Bill's opinion confirmed Lauren's description.

"He didn't come home to Vermont too often, but I saw him a few other times before the accident." Bill's expression grew somber. "That really shook everyone up."

"What happened?" Wes hadn't wanted to question Lauren about the details of Stephen's death.

"Stephen had a reputation for taking risks. He drove too fast, drank too much. The day he died, they say he insisted on skiing off the trail and smashed into a tree going about thirty miles an hour." Lines etched Bill's forehead, and he shook his head slowly. "I don't think he ever knew what hit him."

Conflicting emotions battled within Wes. It didn't seem right for a young man to lose his life like that, but Stephen had hurt Lauren in the worst way. Maybe he deserved what happened to him.

That thought shook Wes. Who was he to condemn another man for his sins? He certainly wasn't sinless. And even if he'd lived a perfect life, how could he judge another man's heart? That was God's job. He would leave the confusing issues of Stephen's guilt and divine justice in God's hands, where they belonged. It was enough for him to know Stephen's death had opened the way for Lauren to return to Vermont. For that he was grateful.

The phone rang. Wes crossed the room to answer it. A woman asked for him by name. He frowned, apprehension straightening his shoulders. He shook it off, certain she must be a telemarketer.

"Are you the Wesley Evans who was an international aid worker and was imprisoned in the Middle East for a year and a half?"

His thoughts raced. Gripping the phone, he scowled. "Who are you?"

"My name's Candice Gallagher. I'm an author

writing a book about modern-day missionaries to the persecuted church. I've read some magazine articles about your experiences, and I'd like to interview you for my book."

"How did you get this number?"

She hesitated a moment, apparently taken aback by his sharp tone. "My aunt works with your mission organization—World Outreach. She told me you'd moved to Tipton, Vermont. I did an Internet search and made a few phone calls. Howard Clarkson gave me your number."

Stunned by how easily she had tracked him down, he glared at Bill and lifted his hand in exasperation.

His friend sent him a confused look. "Who is it?"

Wes shook his head, turned away and paced across the room. He considered telling her she'd found the wrong man, but he couldn't force those words out of his mouth. He'd given up many things when he'd turned his back on his calling as a missionary, but he'd held on to his integrity. He wouldn't lie, not even to protect his privacy.

"I don't want to be interviewed."

"I know it might be difficult for you to recount what you went through, but it would be worth it. My book will raise awareness and motivate people to take a stand for those who are suffering for their faith." Her voice grew more impassioned. "It will broaden prayer support and raise financial donations, and hopefully, it will inspire others to go and serve as you did."

Wes closed his eyes and gripped the back of the

couch, fighting off the wave of guilt that nearly knocked him over. "I'm sorry. I can't help you."

"Please, this is a very important project. I already have interviews with missionaries from China, Indonesia, Thailand, Pakistan, Afghanistan and Tunisia. But your story is unique." She paused for a moment. "You're a hero, Mr. Evans. Everyone who reads my book will understand that. I'm planning to give your story a whole chapter."

Nausea rose and burned his throat. She had no idea what she was asking for. "I'm not interested."

"Would you at least pray about it and take my number?"

He wanted to refuse, but he'd already been rude. It wouldn't hurt to take her phone number. Praying about it was another matter.

He pulled a pen from his shirt pocket and grabbed an old envelope off the end table. "All right. What's your number?" She gave it to him and he scribbled it on the envelope.

"Thanks," she said. "There's no rush. I'm still putting the proposal together. Any time in the next month or so would be fine."

He didn't want to raise her hopes, so he didn't respond. He banged the phone down and turned back to Bill. "I can't believe it!"

"Who was that?"

Wes sank down on the couch. "Some author who wants to interview me for a book she's writing about missionaries."

"How'd she find you?"

"She knows someone at World Outreach. I gave

them my forwarding address a couple weeks ago."
He explained the rest of the trail she'd followed.

Bill crossed his arms. "Howard Clarkson knows
everything about everybody around here. He not
only runs the general store, he's also the post-
master for Tipton."

Wes groaned, remembering how he'd recently
turned in paperwork to open a post office box at
Tipton's general store and post office. He'd answered
all of Howard's friendly questions and thought
nothing of it, including the fact that he was staying
with Bill.

"Don't worry about it. She probably won't call
back."

"Yeah, but if she can find me that easily, so can
everyone else." He stared at the ceiling. "That's all
I need—a clamoring horde of reporters asking me
all kinds of intrusive questions or a gawking bunch
of missionary groupies who have the crazy idea I'm
some kind of hero. There's no way I want to be interviewed."

Wes lowered his head into his hands. "If she knew
what really happened, she wouldn't think I'm a
hero."

"Would that be so bad?"

Wes sighed. "I don't know anymore."

Bill sat down next to Wes. "You put your life on
the line for your faith when you went to the Middle
East. No wonder she wants to write about you."

Wes shook his head. "Believe me, my faith is
nothing worth writing about."

"You're being too hard on yourself. So you had

a few times when you doubted God. Who wouldn't?
They played all kinds of mind games with you. They
threatened and beat you. You didn't know if you
were going to live or die. But you made it through,
and God got you out of there. That's a story worth
telling."

Shame rose like an ugly demon and hovered over
him. *Go on, tell him the rest of the story. See what
he thinks of you then.*

He'd never told Bill how he'd given up hope and
finally signed the confession, explaining his work
and betraying his coworkers and local friends.

"You don't know the half of it," Wes muttered.

"So tell me." His friend's expression reflected
compassion and acceptance.

Wes rubbed his eyes. "Telling you won't change
anything. I just want to forget about it and move on."

Bill sighed. "Okay." He laid his hand on Wes's
shoulder. "Any time you want to talk, I'm here for
you."

Wes fought the stinging sensation in his eyes.
"Thanks," he mumbled as he got up and headed to
his room before the dam burst and his pain poured
out to drown them both.

Chapter Nineteen

Lauren lifted the lid on the spaghetti sauce. The fragrant aroma of basil and oregano floated upward and made her mouth water. She gave the sauce a quick stir, returned the lid and checked the pasta boiling in a tall aluminum pot on the other front burner.

Following Tilley's written directions, she'd managed to avoid any major cooking disasters. Green beans simmered in a small saucepan on the back of the stove. Toasty garlic bread warmed in the oven. A tossed salad chilled in the refrigerator along with a strawberry cheesecake. Hopefully they would entice Wes to accept her dinner invitation—if she could drum up the courage to ask him.

Valentine's Day was almost over and she didn't want to let it pass without doing something special for him.

She bit her lip and glanced at the clock. He and

Toby were due back any minute. Turning, she checked the table set for three. A tall white pillar candle spread a warm glow over the pink tablecloth, the crystal water glasses and Tilley's rose-patterned china.

A nervous tremor traveled up her back. Tilley had left to spend the evening with her friend Eleanor. Lauren had set the third place for Wes, all the while fighting traitorous negative self-talk. What would he think? Was she being too obvious? What if he had other plans?

They hadn't talked much in the past three days since she'd spilled the details of her story. The next afternoon, when Wes had picked up Toby, he'd been quiet, even a little distant. She'd tried to engage him in conversation when he brought her son home, but he only gave her short answers and didn't accept her offer to stay for coffee.

Was he stepping back? Withdrawing from their friendship? Maybe now that he knew the truth, he didn't want to risk his reputation by being involved with someone like her. As that painful thought twisted through her, her stomach tightened into a hard knot.

No, that wasn't the message she'd read in his eyes when she'd poured out her heart to him. He'd wrapped his arms around her as she'd cried. His response had drawn her to him in a deeper way, and the love she had tried to deny grew stronger and filled her with hope.

But how did Wes feel about her? What was he thinking?

Lauren sighed and rubbed her forehead. She ought to stop guessing and simply talk to him. Surely they were mature enough to discuss their relationship and get things out in the open.

If that was true, then why hadn't they? What was she afraid of? What held him back?

Lauren moaned and crossed to the table. If Wes wanted to spend Valentine's Day with her, he would have said so. Pressing him to stay for a romantic dinner wouldn't help the situation. Well, it wouldn't be too romantic with her son seated between them. She snatched the extra plate off the table.

The back door opened and she heard Toby and Wes talking as they stomped the snow from their boots and removed their coats. She spun around to face the table.

Should I put Wes's plate back? Lord, please show me what to do. Three places. She'd already made the decision. Now she just needed to follow through with it. With a trembling hand, she returned Wes's plate to the table.

Toby darted into the kitchen. "Hi, Mom." The cold air had tinged his cheeks and nose pink. "Look, I made you something." Grinning, he pulled a piece of folded white paper from behind his back.

Wes stepped into the kitchen. Lauren looked up. His gaze connected with hers. His eyes glowed with mischief and just a touch of some other emotion she couldn't quite read.

"Mom, it's a valentine!" Toby grabbed her arm, waving the paper back and forth like an excited butterfly on a breezy day. "You have to read it!"

She laughed at his enthusiasm and accepted the card. Slipping her arm around his shoulders, she quickly scanned the words written in red marker. Though several letters had been scribbled out and written a second time, the message was clear and flew straight to her heart.

To Mom, Happy Valentine's Day.

Warm tendrils of pleasure wrapped themselves around her as she read the words.

I love you very much. You are the best mom in the world.

She blinked away happy tears and pulled him in for a tight hug. "Thank you, Toby. That's very special." Squeezing him tightly, she planted a kiss on his cheek.

"Wes told me how to spell some words, but I wrote it myself." Toby wiggled out of her arms, pride in his accomplishment wreathing his face with joy.

"I love it. I'm going to put it right here on the fridge." Scooting aside his drawing of an eagle, she secured the precious valentine with two magnets.

Lauren turned and faced Wes, gratitude and affection bubbled up in her heart. The time he invested in her son's life, the lessons of kindness and caring he taught him…no one else had ever touched their lives like that.

Wes smiled at her, a renewed warmth and openness in his expression.

Casting aside her doubts, she asked, "Can you stay for dinner?"

A hopeful light flickered in his eyes. He glanced at the table and his expression clouded over. "Ah, that's okay. You're all set. You don't have to move it around to make room for—"

"No, I want you to stay. Tilley's away tonight… I set that place for you." She felt her cheeks flush, and she ran a nervous hand over her black jeans. "If you have other plans, that's okay. I understand." Her stomach did a crazy somersault as he looked intently at her.

His smile returned. "No, I don't have anything else going on tonight. I'd love to stay. Thanks." He chuckled, looking relieved. "Dinner smells great, and we're starving, aren't we, Toby?" He grabbed her son around the shoulders and ruffled the hair on top of his head.

Toby grinned up at Wes. "Yeah, what's for dinner, Mom?"

"I made your favorite—spaghetti."

Toby hooted his approval. Lauren sent him to wash his hands. Wes took off his jacket, hung it over the back of a chair, then followed Toby to the kitchen sink where they continued to tease each other as they washed up. Soon they were seated around the table, the flicker of candlelight on each face. Lauren smiled at the special men in her life, thankful to share Valentine's Day with them.

Wes stirred cream into his coffee as he watched Lauren slice him a large piece of cheesecake, topped with brightly glazed strawberries. His mouth began to water and he wasn't sure if it was the promised dessert or the vision of the beautiful lady who had delighted and captured his heart. Probably both.

Lauren had never looked more attractive. Her soft blue sweater and neat black jeans showed off her slim, feminine figure. She'd left her long hair down with no braid or ponytail to rein in its bronze glory. It flowed over her shoulders in shiny waves.

She looked…beautiful, not like a fashion model or movie star who wore tons of makeup and had plastic surgery to perfect every tiny flaw, but more like a field of wildflowers or a stunning sunset. Her beauty started in her heart and shined through her eyes and smile. It was reflected in her sweet, caring spirit, drawing him like a high-powered magnet. Even when he wasn't with her he could hardly think of anything else.

She looked up and sent him a heart-stopping smile as she passed him his dessert plate. "Hope you like strawberries."

"I love 'em." He took a bite and let the creamy delight melt in his mouth. "Mmm, delicious!" He closed his eyes and sighed, savoring the perfect blend of fresh, sweet strawberries and cool, rich cheesecake.

She laughed, obviously enjoying his response. After pouring herself a steaming cup of coffee, she sat down across from him with a smaller slice of cheesecake.

He took a sip from his mug and studied her face, mesmerized by the soft sweep of her dark lashes and her soft cheeks. His gaze settled on her coral lips.

They tipped up in a small smile as she glanced at him and then back at her plate.

Suddenly, the memory of the kiss they had shared filled his mind, evoking a powerful replay of the moment.

He shifted his eyes away, cleared his throat and frowned at his coffee cup.

"Everything okay?" She tilted her head, looking concerned.

"Yeah, sure. Everything's fine." He sent her a quick glance and scooped up another bite of cheesecake. If he wanted God to honor their growing relationship, he had to keep his thoughts in line, no matter how much memories of the past and present tempted him.

He'd spent the past couple of days praying about his feelings for Lauren, asking for confirmation and clear direction. His heart told him yes, it was time to take the next step and move ahead, but he wanted to be certain he was following the Lord's leading and not just his own. Tonight's special dinner and the sweet looks she had been sending him all evening gave him an extra shot of courage and confidence.

Lauren carved off the tiniest bite of cheesecake and slipped it into her mouth. Sighing, she settled back in her chair looking perfectly content. "This is really good."

He grinned. "You sound surprised."

"I am. This is the first time I've tried this recipe."

"You're kidding. It's great. I thought it was an old family favorite."

"Well, Tilley makes it all the time…so I know how it's supposed to taste…and this is pretty close." She wrinkled her nose and grinned.

She looked adorable. He laughed, tickled by her honest humor.

Toby filled his mouth with another big bite of cheesecake and gobbled it down like there was no tomorrow.

Lauren sent her son an indulgent smile. "Slow down and enjoy it, Toby. At least take time to taste it as it's going down."

An impish grin lit up Toby's face. "I can taste it. It's good."

Wes smiled and winked at Lauren. He couldn't deny it. His feelings for her ran deep. He couldn't imagine spending the future with anyone else. The fact that Toby was part of her life only made it a sweeter deal. This sense of connection and longing to share his life with her filled him with optimism and purpose.

He loved her. The thought raced through him, burning a trail straight to his heart. He'd do anything to protect her, even lay down his life if he had to.

Would he really? Doubt swept over him as scenes from prison flashed in his mind. Once again, loneliness and pain tore at his soul. Remembering his struggle to hold on to his faith and the anguish he experienced as he signed his confession, a shudder passed through him.

Was he capable of loving her as she deserved?

He pulled in a deep breath, shook off those fears and focused on Lauren's lovely face. He'd never be in a situation like that again or face another drastic choice with such great consequences, but he could lay down his pride and his fear of having his past exposed so that he and Lauren could build a life together.

Tonight he'd tell her the truth and see if she could ever love a man who had such a long way to go to rebuild his life and take hold of his future.

He heard the back door open, and Tilley called a greeting. Seconds later she bustled into the kitchen.

"Would you like some dessert?" Lauren asked.

"Oh, no thanks, dear, but I'd love a cup of coffee."

Lauren crossed to the cupboard and retrieved a coffee mug for her aunt.

Wes sighed and laid down his fork. There went his chance for a quiet evening alone with Lauren. He forced a smile and greeted Tilley.

"Wes, did you know you left your truck engine running?" Tilley walked toward the kitchen table. "The light's on inside the cab, too."

Wes shifted in his seat. "Thanks, I'll take care of that in a minute."

Lauren set Tilley's coffee cup on the table. "Go ahead, Wes. I don't want you to run out of gas."

"Well, I…have something in there and I don't want it to freeze."

Lauren lifted her brows and looked at him curiously.

Wes wiped his mouth with a napkin and stood up. "Will you come with me?"

She blinked once, surprise written in her large blue eyes. Then an inquisitive smile spread across her lips. "Okay."

He grabbed his coat from the back of the chair and pulled it on.

Toby jumped up. "I want to come."

Wes sent him a serious look. "I'm sorry, but not this time, buddy."

Tilley laid her hand on Toby's shoulder. "We'll be fine. You two go ahead."

Wes quickly placed his hand on the small of Lauren's back and guided her toward the door before she could object. "Here, you'll need your coat." He pulled her green wool jacket off the hook and held it out for her.

She slipped her arms in the sleeves and looked up at him, delight shining in her eyes. "What's going on?"

"Come on, you'll see." He took her hand and led her out the door and down the icy steps. Her hand felt small and warm, a perfect fit. Moonlight painted deep blue shadows across the snowy yard, but the path to the driveway was clear. He'd taken care of that this afternoon.

When they reached the truck, he stopped and turned to her. "Close your eyes."

She laughed. "What?"

"You heard me. Close your eyes and climb in." He swallowed, suddenly feeling more nervous than a teenager on his first date. Was he jumping the gun?

"What are you up to?" She tried to look bothered, but her tone and sparkling eyes told her true feelings. She loved surprises. He knew it.

"It's Valentine's Day. You don't want to spoil this, do you?"

"Oh, sorry." She obediently shut her eyes and climbed into the passenger seat, a smile twitching at the corners of her mouth.

"Okay, I'm going around to the other side. Keep your eyes closed and wait for me." He shut her door, hustled around the front of the truck and climbed into the driver's seat. With one last nervous glance at her expectant face, he placed his surprise in her lap and scooted closer.

Chapter Twenty

Lauren kept her eyes closed. The surprise on her lap wasn't heavy, but its flat, smooth surface spread across both her legs. She felt Wes's warm breath on her cheek as he moved closer. A shiver of delight raced through her.

"Okay, you can look now."

Her eyes flew open and she gasped. A long gold box tied with a bright red ribbon lay on her lap. The words Richard's Flowers were imprinted on top.

"Happy Valentine's Day." Warmth glowed in Wes's eyes, along with just a hint of apprehension.

She smiled and reached to hug him. "Thank you, Wes." She leaned into his embrace, and her cheek rested against his scratchy wool coat. It smelled faintly of wood smoke and Wes's icy, fresh aftershave. The tantalizing combination stirred memories of other times she'd been close enough to catch the scent that was uniquely Wes.

He chuckled. "You're welcome, but you haven't even opened the box to see what's inside."

"I know, but it's just…" Unexpected tears gathered in her eyes. She leaned back and looked into his handsome face. "This is so sweet. No one's ever given me flowers."

He slipped his arm around her shoulder and pulled her closer, giving her a few seconds to collect herself. "You ready to look inside?"

She smiled and nodded, then slipped off the ribbon and lifted the lid. A dazzling bouquet of long-stemmed red roses and white baby's breath lay on a bed of dark green ferns.

"Oh, Wes, they're so beautiful." She bent forward and sniffed, catching their wonderful fragrance. "I love roses."

Her chin wobbled. She reached up and whisked away a hot tear from her cheek, but that didn't stop the flow. Her joy swirled away in a sea of confusion and uncertainty. Why was she acting like a blubbering child?

Wes's dark brows drew together, and concern filled his eyes. "Hey, those aren't happy tears. What's going on? Did I do something wrong?"

"No, it's not you. It's me." She waved her hand at the lovely bouquet. "I just don't understand why you're giving me flowers."

He frowned slightly. "Well, this is Valentine's Day. Isn't that what a guy is supposed to do for the special girl in his life?"

"Yes, but I'm not…I mean, you're… Oh, this is so confusing."

"You can say that again." He scanned her face, looking perplexed.

"I'm sorry." She sniffed and rummaged in her coat pocket until she found a rumpled tissue. Raising it to her drippy nose, she blew. Wes had gone out of his way to buy her flowers, and not just any flowers but a very expensive Valentine's Day bouquet, and she was crying and acting like she didn't want them.

He sighed and closed his eyes for several seconds. Finally, he opened them and tightened his arm around her shoulders. "Lauren, I'm sorry. I went about this all wrong. I should have explained myself first instead of springing these flowers on you and expecting you to guess what I'm thinking."

She pressed her lips together and tried to rein in her tumultuous emotions. Now she was really going to cry.

He raised her hand to his lips and placed a feathery kiss on top. "You're very special to me, and I want you to know how I feel about you."

She clutched her wadded tissue more tightly. How could he be so sweet to her when he knew the awful details of her past? "But Wes, I'm not…"

"Not what?" Now he looked even more confused.

"I'm not like you." She sniffed. "You're good and kind and caring. And I've never met anyone so…spiritual. It's just a little intimidating."

He stared at her, looking crestfallen. "Wow, I've never been rejected for being too spiritual."

"I'm not rejecting you. I'm just trying to figure

out why a guy like you would want a relationship with someone like me." She felt her face flush, but she continued to look him in the eyes. "I told you what happened with Stephen."

"Lauren, that was a long time ago."

"But I have a son. That's never going to change."

"But Toby turned out to be a blessing in your life, and the struggles you went through opened your eyes to your need for a relationship with Jesus."

"That doesn't change the fact that there's a stigma attached to being a single parent. People make assumptions about me all the time, and if you and I get…involved, then it will affect how people look at you, too."

A stubborn glint lit his eyes. "I'm not worried about what people think. What happened between you and Stephen is in the past. You weren't a Christian then. Now you are. The Bible says when you accept Christ as your savior, you become a new and different person. Your sins are forgiven. You get a fresh start, a new family and a new future."

Though his words sounded wonderful, doubt dampened her spirit. "I don't feel new and different. What happened with Stephen is still so…huge to me." She swallowed and forced herself to speak. "I know God forgives sins, and I've confessed it over and over, but I still don't feel forgiven." Her voice came out in a sorrowful whisper.

Wes nodded thoughtfully and rubbed his thumb over the top of her hand. Then he looked into her eyes. "It's one thing to know God forgives sins, it's another to believe you are truly and completely forgiven. That takes faith in God and His Word, and understanding what Christ's death on the cross accomplished for us."

He reached into his coat pocket and pulled out a small brown leather Bible. "Here, listen to this verse. 'For as high as the heavens are above the earth, so great is His love for those who fear Him, as far as the east is from the west, so far has He removed our transgressions from us.'"

Assurance flowed from his eyes. "Your sins are wiped away, paid for by Christ's death. You don't have to carry them around anymore." He squeezed her hand. "Let them go, Lauren. Accept God's forgiveness and open your heart to the peace and freedom He wants you to enjoy."

Lauren leaned on Wes's chest and closed her eyes. "I want to believe that more than anything."

He wrapped his arms around her. "That's all God is looking for, a willing heart. Can I pray for you?"

She nodded.

Wes ran his hand gently down her hair and closed his eyes. "Father, please give Lauren grace to accept Your forgiveness. Remind her of the truth in Your Word and help her move ahead and take hold of all You have planned for her. In Jesus' name, amen."

Lauren whispered amen with Wes. Nestled safely in his arms, she found it easier to believe God's healing promises.

Wes stroked Lauren's silky hair. Wonder and thanksgiving overflowed his heart. Not only did he hold Lauren in his arms, he'd finally been able to share the truth about God's forgiveness for her painful past. Since the first day they met, he knew she carried a burden only God could lift…but she needed someone she trusted to show her the way. So many times he'd prayed for that opportunity. Tonight, his prayer had been answered. He smiled, positive, hopeful feelings swelling his chest. This was just the beginning.

"Thank you, Wes." She leaned back and gazed at him with adoring eyes and a tremulous smile.

"You're welcome." He gently tucked a wayward strand of hair behind her ear, wanting to tell her how much he loved her. But he didn't want to over-whelm her or distract her from the important work God was doing in her heart.

"I've heard those verses before," she said softly, "but I never understood how I needed to believe and accept God's forgiveness. I guess I've paid more attention to my feelings than I have to the truth."

He pulled her closer and rested his chin on top of her head, relishing the moment. "Come on, I better get you inside before you freeze."

Reluctantly, he let her go and climbed out of the truck. The frosty air stung his nose as he walked around to open Lauren's door. She held the box of flowers, so he reached for her arm and helped her down.

She smiled her thanks, then stopped and stared over his shoulder. "Oh Wes, look!"

He turned, scanning the driveway and path to the house. "What?"

"Not down there. Look up." She laughed and

pointed to the sky. Then she tucked her arm through his and snuggled closer.

Lifting his gaze, he saw a shimmering curtain of light hanging in the northern sky. "Wow, that's amazing." He tilted his head back, watching the glowing bands of soft green and silver dance above the trees in a hypnotic rhythm.

"Have you ever seen the northern lights before?" She leaned on his arm, her voice soft and dreamy.

"Once, in Norway." As soon as the words left his mouth, he stiffened.

She turned and searched his face. "When did you go to Norway?"

Here was his opportunity. He could tell her everything—explain his years as a missionary, his imprisonment, his stay at La Ruche and his travels through Europe.

"Wes?" She looked up at him, her eyes reflecting the shimmering lights.

"The past couple of years have been a difficult time for me," he said in a halting voice. His heart thundered, and he felt like he stood on the edge of a cliff, about to fall off into the darkness. How could he explain what he'd done? Hadn't she just said he was good and kind and spiritual? She admired his faith. If she knew the truth about him, would she reject what he'd just told her about God's forgiveness? He coughed and cleared his throat, still torn by his internal debate.

"Last fall I spent some time in Switzerland. I toured around Germany and Denmark, and then traveled through Sweden and Norway. That was right before I came here." His shoulders sagged with a mixture of relief and disappointment. At least he'd opened the door a crack and told her something.

"Wow. Which country did you like the best?" She smiled, looking unaware of his struggle.

"Switzerland was great. I hiked through the Alps for a couple weeks, trying to sort things out and re-connect with God." He paused and stared at the fading lights. "I guess I was really looking for peace and a place to call home."

"Did you find it?" she asked softly.

"No…not until I came here and met you." He pulled her into his embrace. "Oh, Lauren." A huge lump lodged in his throat, and tears burned in his eyes.

Go on, tell her the rest. It's not too late.

Don't be a fool. She'd never love a coward.

His thoughts snarled into a tangled mess like fishing line caught in a tree. He closed his heart to the debate.

Not now. Not tonight.

But hiding behind half-truths was the same as telling a lie. How could he do that to the woman he loved?

Chapter Twenty-One

Lauren glanced up from the gallery inventory lists overflowing on her lap. Her gaze drifted toward the couch, where Wes sat next to Toby, reading a story aloud. Her son leaned against Wes's side, totally absorbed in the tale of Homer Price cranking out hundreds of doughnuts and searching for a missing diamond bracelet.

Wes read with wonderful expression, using different voices for the characters, delighting her son and drawing her into the story as well. Wes paused and laughed at a funny line. Toby giggled along with him.

Across from Wes, Tilley sat with her slipper-clad feet up on a footstool. She chuckled too, her knitting needles never slowing as she continued to work on a baby sweater for a new arrival in their church family.

The fire crackled and the scent of Tilley's fresh-baked cinnamon rolls hung in the air. They'd enjoyed those sticky, sweet delights earlier with cups of coffee for the adults and hot cocoa for Toby.

The scene warmed Lauren all the way to her toes. These were precious times. Since Valentine's Day, Wes often stayed for dinner after his time spent with Toby. Then last Saturday, he'd helped her finish the bathroom in her barn-turned-gallery. On Sunday he'd taken them out for lunch at the Chinese restaurant in West Harmon. And later that day, he'd teamed up with Bill to move some large pieces of antique furniture into the gallery so she could begin setting up displays.

Long Meadow Art and Antique Gallery was set to open on March twenty-first, the first day of spring, a little over two weeks away. Though Lauren's list of unfinished tasks looked daunting, with Wes's help she just might make it.

Wes read the final line and closed the book.

"Read it again," Toby begged, tugging on Wes's arm.

"I'm glad you like it, but I think it's about your bedtime, buddy."

"That's right," Lauren added as she stifled a yawn.

Toby moaned. "But I'm not tired. Why do I have to go to bed now?"

"It's a school night. You know the rule."

He slowly pulled himself up off the couch with a little help from Wes. Lauren set aside her paperwork and rose from her chair.

"I'm headed upstairs. I'll tuck Toby in." Tilley

poked her needles into the ball of soft blue yarn and tucked it in her bag. "Come on, sweetie."

Toby gave slow, sleepy hugs to Wes and Lauren and then followed Tilley upstairs without any more complaints. Bryn lifted her head and watched Toby go, thumped her tail once and laid her head back down on the hearth.

Wes smiled and held out his hand to Lauren. "Come here." His dark eyes twinkled.

She rose from her chair, a smile on her lips. With a contented sigh, she settled on the couch next to him.

He slipped his arm around her shoulder. "I have some good news."

"What?" She turned and studied his face.

"I bought a car." He lifted his dark brows, awaiting her reaction.

"Wow, really?" Hope filled her heart. This meant he was settling down, getting established.

He nodded, looking pleased. "I am now the proud owner of a used, late-model, blue, four-door, automatic modern mode of transportation."

She laughed, enjoying his lighthearted mood. "So…tell me how it happened."

"One of the guys at work bought a new SUV and he wanted to sell his other car. So Bill and I took it for a test-drive. We negotiated a great price, and the car is now mine." His eyes shone as though he had won a prize.

"That's great. Is it parked out back? I can't believe you waited so long to show me." She started to get up, but he took her hand and pulled her back.

His expression deflated a little. "I can't drive it until tomorrow. I have to give him the rest of the money, sign the papers and get my insurance."

She squeezed his hand. "We'll celebrate tomorrow, then."

"That's exactly what I was thinking." He wrapped a strand of her hair around his finger and pulled her closer until only a few inches separated their faces. "How about I pick you up and take you for a drive in my new car and then we fix dinner at my house?"

Her heart did a funny little dance. "Sounds fun." Her thoughts skipped ahead. "Maybe I could ask Tilley to watch Toby." She felt a little awkward making the suggestion, but it would be good for them to have some time alone.

Wes's gaze warmed. "He's welcome to come, but an evening with just you and me sounds nice."

"Okay. I'll ask her." She hesitated a second. "What about Bill?"

"He's busy."

"You asked him already?"

"No, but I'll make sure he has other plans." Wes grinned.

She laughed and reached up to kiss his cheek. "That's very sweet."

"Sweet?" He looked chagrined.

"Thoughtful?"

"How about romantic?" That twinkle was back in his eyes as he leaned closer.

"Okay…romantic." Her eyes slid closed, and he gave her a kiss sweeter than cinnamon rolls and hot cocoa.

* * *

Lauren accepted her change, thanked the clerk and wrapped the yellow ribbon around her hand twice. She didn't want to lose the happy-face Mylar balloon before she left the store. Clutching her shopping bag in the other hand, she walked toward the door, the balloon bobbing along behind her.

She planned to tie the balloon to the antenna of Wes's new car, attach a huge red bow to the hood, wrap his steering wheel with a new black leather cover and hang one of those funny little pine-tree air fresheners from his rearview mirror. Bill had managed to get her an extra car key so she could pull off her surprise.

Glancing at her watch, she quickened her pace. Wes got off in thirty minutes. She'd have to hurry. Pushing open the heavy glass door, she looked over her shoulder to be sure the balloon followed her out safely.

"Hello, Lauren."

The male voice startled her and she spun around.

Ryan Zeller smiled as he held the door open. "Looks like you're headed to a party."

"Not really." Flustered, she reeled in the ribbon on the balloon. Seeing him made her feel like a bucket of cold water had been dumped on her head, dousing her happiness.

"So is the balloon for Toby?"

The door whooshed closed behind her. The mention of her son sent a shiver up her back. "No." She turned to go, but he stepped into her path. Her gaze darted past his shoulder, searching the chilly, vacant street. Though cars lined both sides, not a soul was in sight.

"I've been looking for you at Wild River. I was hoping you and Toby would come for those ski lessons."

She fiddled with her bag. "I've been busy."

"Right." He nodded, sending her a skeptical smile. "How about Saturday? Name the time. I'm free all day."

Gripping her shopping bag tighter, she tried to calm her sprinting pulse. "Look, Ryan. I appreciate the passes, but I don't think we'll be using them. My gallery opens in a couple of weeks. I have a lot to do to get everything ready. I really don't have time—"

"With all the trouble Toby's having at school, maybe you ought to reconsider and adjust your busy schedule." Sarcasm tinged his words.

Anger bristled her nerves. "Who said Toby's having trouble at school?"

He laughed. "I can find out whatever I want to know about anyone in this town."

Her face flushed. "Well, how Toby's doing at school is none of your business."

"It is if he's my nephew."

Lauren froze and stared at him, her heart tumbling to her feet.

"Why do you look so surprised? The family resemblance is strong. Along with that and a little basic math, it's not hard to figure out. Stephen was Toby's father, right?"

"I—I don't have to answer that." She pushed past him.

He caught up and matched her hurried steps. "Don't run away. I want to help you." He reached for her arm.

She jerked back. The balloon slipped from her fingers. Floating upward, its yellow ribbon dangled just out of reach. She lunged for it, but the wind whipped it from her fingers. Disheartened, she turned away and kept walking.

Ryan kept pace with her. "Toby deserves a chance for a better life. He doesn't need to struggle like this. I'll pay for the best private school, tutoring or whatever he needs. He's a Zeller."

Fear coiled around her throat. Her steps faltered. Then she shook her head and pressed on. "I don't want your help," she whispered fiercely.

He grabbed her arm and pulled her to a stop. "I'm going to manage Wild River. I'll be able to hire and fire whomever I want, including employees at the Nature Center."

His veiled threat knocked the wind from her. She gulped in a breath, fighting her rising fear. She couldn't let Wes lose his job just because she was too proud to acknowledge Stephen was Toby's father. Ryan already suspected the truth. What sense was there in pretending it wasn't so? Lifting her chin, she looked Ryan in the eyes. "What do you want from me?"

He slid his hand down her arm as he took a step closer. "I want a chance to show you I'm not like Stephen." Ryan reached up and fingered a strand of her hair. "You're a very beautiful woman, Lauren."

Ryan's manic mood shift sent a dizzy wave of

panic through her. She swallowed and forced herself to get a grip and think clearly. "Ryan, listen. It doesn't matter to me what your last name is, how much money you have or even what you want to do for Toby. In order for two people to be together, they have to feel a special connection and be—"

He scowled. "You're in love with Wes Evans. That's why you're not interested in me."

"That has nothing to do with it."

"Yes, it does. If he was out of the picture, you'd see things differently."

"You can't expect to build a relationship with someone by bribing and threatening them."

"Give me a chance, Lauren. I could give you and Toby everything you've ever wanted."

Exasperated, she lifted her hands. "You're not listening to me." She stepped away from him.

"Don't do it, Lauren." His voice was low and threatening.

Goose bumps rose on her arms. Her steps stalled and she turned around. "Don't do what?"

"Don't walk away from me like this." His painful expression almost made her feel sorry for him. Was it real or contrived to get a response?

Weary and uncertain, she let out a deep sigh. "Ryan, I'm not walking away from anything. We don't have a relationship, or even a friendship."

Anger flared in his eyes, replacing the look of sadness. Glaring, he turned and stalked off.

Chapter Twenty-Two

Wes scooted Bill's stuffed raccoon to the left as he searched through the papers on top of the Nature Center filing cabinet. He thought he'd seen the sign-up sheet for Saturday's bird-watching trek up there yesterday.

"Here it is," Bill called as he walked back into the office. "I left it in the kitchen when I went to get some coffee earlier."

"Good. Now at least we'll know how many people to expect." Wes reached for his coffee mug, took a sip and glanced out the window. A fresh blanket of snow covered the woods surrounding the Nature Center, bringing the total to about seven inches. But that wouldn't stop the hearty group of bird-watching enthusiasts who donned snowshoes for their annual winter trek through the woods.

Bill sat down at his desk. "So how's the new car running?"

"Great." Wes settled on the corner of Bill's desk, picked up the sign-up sheet and scanned the names.

"How was your special dinner with Lauren?"

"Nice." Wes grinned and took another sip of coffee.

"That's all you're gonna tell me?"

"Yep."

"No fair. I had to spend the whole evening in Walt's garage listening to those same stories he always tells so you could have the house to yourself. I should at least get some details."

"Sorry. You gotta stop trying to live your life vicariously through me. Get your own girlfriend."

Bill laughed. "Yeah, like I can just snap my fingers and make her appear."

The phone rang and Bill reached to answer it. After a quick greeting, he shifted his gaze to Wes. "Okay. I'll tell him." A slight frown creased his forehead as he hung up the phone. "That was Jeanne in the main office. She said Mr. Zeller wants to see you right away."

An uneasy ripple raised the hair on the back of Wes's neck. "I wonder what he wants."

Concern filled Bill's eyes. "I don't know."

Wes shook off his uneasiness. "He probably wants to give me a raise or offer me full-time hours."

"Hope so. You're doing a good job, and I could use you every day."

Wes grabbed his coat off the hook on the back of Bill's door. "Guess I'll head over there and find out what he wants."

Bill slapped his shoulder. "Don't worry. I'll shoot a prayer up for you."

"Thanks." Wes nodded, glad Bill's prayers would cover the meeting.

Three minutes later, Wes knocked on Arthur Zeller's door.

"Come in," the voice called from the office.

Wes opened the door and stalled on the threshold. He clenched his jaw, staring at the man who had summoned him. Ryan Zeller leaned back in his father's large black leather chair and propped his feet up on his father's desk.

"Shut the door and have a seat." Ryan steepled his fingers in front of his mouth and studied Wes with a calculating look.

Wes crossed the office and took a seat opposite Ryan, his senses on alert and his mind sifting through all the possible reasons for this meeting. He hadn't seen Ryan since Lauren's birthday party almost a month ago. He'd hoped Ryan had finally given up his pursuit of Lauren. But this summons didn't bode well.

"I suppose you're wondering why I called you in."

Wes held his gaze but didn't speak.

Ryan lowered his feet and faced Wes. "It looks like you weren't honest with us on your job application. That's a serious problem."

"What are you talking about?"

"Our reputation as a safe, family-friendly resort is important to us. We only want to employ people who have good character and can be trusted, especially in the Nature Center where children are involved."

Wes gripped the arm of the chair. "Are you implying there's some reason I shouldn't be working with kids?"

Ryan opened a file and slid the application across the desk toward Wes. "In the section where you listed your previous employment, you wrote that you held various odd jobs as you traveled through Europe last August through December." He looked up at Wes. "Is that correct?"

"Yes."

"Below that you said you were a teacher in the city of Esfahan. But the dates you gave leave an eighteen-month gap between that job and your travels through Europe. What were you doing during that time?"

Wes shifted in his chair, his apprehension rising. "I wasn't working then."

"What were you doing?"

"You asked for my employment history. That's what I gave you."

Ryan sat back. "Sometimes, information left out tells more about a person than what they write down."

What was going on? Was this a test to see if he would tell the truth, or was it some kind of mind game? If he played along could he save his job? Sickening memories of his interrogations by the prison officials flashed in his mind. His heart pounded and sweat broke out on his forehead. He closed his eyes and took a deep breath. This was Vermont, not the Middle East. He was a free man, not a prisoner. All he needed to do was tell the truth and answer Ryan's question. Once he explained his imprisonment, everything would be okay.

He looked up. "For six years I was a missionary in the Middle East, working for an international aid organization called World Outreach. I ran a small medical clinic in Karandar for three years, and I taught street children in Esfahan for a year and a half. I listed both those jobs on my application." He pointed to the form and turned it for Ryan to see. "Then, two years ago, I was arrested for teaching Bible stories to the children in our program. Evangelism is illegal there, so I spent eighteen months in prison. I was released last August."

"You were accused of working for the CIA."

Wes snorted. "That's what they think about every American who spends time in their country."

Ryan raised his brows as though he didn't believe Wes's explanation.

"What?" Wes huffed. "You think I'm some kind of spy?"

"They held you for eighteen months and tried you in their courts."

Wes banged his hand on the desk. "That so-called trial was a mockery! My lawyer barely spoke English. The only thing I'm guilty of was sharing the Gospel with poor street kids who needed to know God loves them."

"Well, that certainly sounds heroic. But what concerns me are the reports about your mental state while you were in prison. The article in *Newsweek* said you suffered an emotional breakdown. A religious magazine called it a crisis of faith." He looked directly at Wes. "What would you call it?"

"I'd call it over and done with." Seething at Ryan's audacity, Wes rose from his chair.

"Sit down, Wes. We need to finish this conversation."

"Why, so you can belittle me and then fire me? No thanks." He strode across the office and reached for the doorknob.

"You haven't told Lauren any of this, have you?" It wasn't a question but a statement, heavy with accusation.

His hand froze and a stabbing pain shot through his chest. He turned and glared at Ryan. "That's none of your business."

"You're wrong. Lauren and I have been friends for years. In fact, Toby is my nephew." Ryan paused, watching, as though he wanted to gauge Wes's reaction.

Wes stared at him coldly, not giving him the satisfaction of any response.

Ryan leaned forward, his expression intent. "I don't want your history causing us problems, and I don't want Lauren or Toby hurt by someone who's dishonest and unstable."

"You know nothing about me except what you've read in some magazine articles. The reporters who write those stories don't care about the truth. They just want to create a sensation and sell more magazines." Wes walked back to the desk and leaned both hands on top. "I'd never hurt Lauren and Toby.

I'm perfectly stable, and I've explained more than you deserve to know to prove my honesty."

Ryan leaned back and crossed his arms. "Sorry, Wes. I don't believe you." His cool expression showed no true sorrow; instead, a hint of triumph shone in his eyes.

"If you leave town quietly, without contacting Lauren, I'll keep this to myself. I'll even give you a letter of recommendation so you can get another job somewhere else."

Wes narrowed his eyes, barely able to hold back the fury building inside. "You'd like that, wouldn't you? Get me out of the way so you can move in on Lauren. Forget it. I'll tell Lauren the truth, and I know she won't have any trouble believing me."

"Maybe, maybe not. But when I put the word out to the media where to find you, she might be sorry she ever got involved with you."

"Why, you—" Wes swallowed the words forming on his tongue, but his anger roiled like a boiling pot. "You might be able to fire me, but I'm not leaving town. I love Lauren, and nothing you do or say is going to change that."

"Do you really love her, Wes?"

"Yes!"

"Then pack your bags and leave Tipton."

"No! I don't care who you tell about my past. I'm not leaving Lauren and Toby."

"If you don't leave, I'll not only call in the media and destroy your reputation, I'll go to court to prove Lauren is an unfit mother and take custody of Toby."

Wes stared at him, his blood running cold. "You

could never prove that. She loves Toby. She's doing a great job with him."

"When you have money to hire a high-powered lawyer and just a few hints of trouble, you can prove anything you want." He opened another file and slid several pictures across the desk toward Wes.

Wes's eyes burned as he stared at the photos. The first showed Toby crying as Lauren tugged him toward the waiting school bus, her face stern with determination. The next captured a shot of Lauren painting her gallery late at night. The third pictured Toby in tears, clinging to his school yard's chain-link fence. And the fourth was a close-up shot of Lauren kissing Wes the day they'd cross-country skied through Bower's Creek State Park.

"You were the photographer who tracked us!" Wes snatched the pictures off the desk. "These prove nothing! There's an explanation for every one of these photos."

Ryan shrugged. "Our lawyer says Lauren's pre-occupation with her new business, Toby's trouble at school, her live-in relationship with you and the way she tried to hide his true identity from our family is enough to give us a strong case. Even without the photos, we'll easily win custody."

"Why?" Pain scorched his voice. "Why would you hurt her like this?"

"Oh, I won't. You'll be the one to bring all of this down on her head if you don't leave town."

So this was how the game was played. If he stayed, Ryan would take Toby away and devastate Lauren. She could never be happy in a relationship with Wes knowing his selfish desire to be with her had caused her to lose her son.

But if he left, he would lose Lauren, the only woman he had ever loved. How could he give her up? If he walked away without giving her some kind of explanation, she would be left wounded and wondering. But would that be worse than losing her son? No. She might miss Wes for a few weeks, but her relationship with Toby was more important than a fleeting romance with him.

"You say you love her." Ryan stood up behind the desk. "If that's true, then you only have one choice. Let her go."

Wes's gaze darted from Ryan's icy-blue eyes to the photos on the desk. Was he bluffing? Would he really follow through and try to take Toby away from Lauren? What if Wes stayed and they fought him? No, the stakes were too high. His longings for love and family were not worth the risk of losing that battle.

He had to concede the fight and sacrifice his own desires. That was the only way to protect Lauren and Toby.

He leveled his gaze at Ryan. "If I leave, you give me your word you'll drop this plan to pursue custody of Toby?"

"Yes." Ryan lifted his chin and his lips thinned in a slight smile. "As long as you agree you won't initiate any contact with Lauren now or in the future." He glanced at his watch. "Pick up your check and letter of recommendation from me tomorrow on your way out of town. Agreed?"

Pain swamped him like waves crashing over a drowning man's head. He nodded and strode out of the office.

Toby leaned on the front windowsill, tears rolling down his cheeks. He wiped his nose on his sleeve and looked up at Lauren. "Why didn't he come? He promised to take me skating. We had it all planned."

Lauren handed him a tissue and laid her hand on his shoulder. "I don't know, sweetie."

"Call him again," Toby pleaded. "It's not too late. We could still go if he hurries."

Lauren shook her head, fighting her own feelings of frustration. "I already left two messages. He must've had car trouble or something. I'm sure he'll call and explain as soon as he can."

Toby sniffed and stuck out his lower lip. "Yeah, but by then it will be too late to go."

Her son was right. There would be no skating trip tonight. Lauren pulled Toby close and they hugged each other. Oh, if only she could hug away all the pain she had caused him by bringing him into the world without a father.

Tears misted her eyes as she glanced over his shoulder at the lavender sunset fading into the indigo evening sky. The clouds shifted and a tiny star blinked at her. Within seconds, the light disappeared as new, threatening clouds moved in.

Uneasiness settled over her heart. Wes had not only promised to take Toby skating, he'd said he would come for dinner and then help her hang quilts in the gallery tonight. It wasn't like him to let them both down like this. In the past he'd always called if he was going to be late. Something was wrong.

The urge to pray rose and stormed her heart. She trembled and closed her eyes, drawing close the One she was learning to turn to whenever she felt afraid. *Father, watch over Wes. Keep him safe. Let us hear from him soon. Help me trust You to take care of him and lead him safely home.*

Chapter Twenty-Three

Lauren circled the Nature Center's parking lot a second time, searching for an empty spot. Saturday mornings were usually busy at Wild River, but this was ridiculous. Gripping the steering wheel, she drove up the next aisle and continued her search for a vacant spot.

She had lain awake until after midnight worrying about Wes. Why hadn't he called back and explained his absence? It was bad enough he'd stood her up last night but he'd also disappointed her son and left him in tears. That was almost unforgivable.

Wes Evans had some explaining to do.

This morning she'd hoped to catch him at home, but when she drove by, she found his driveway empty. She didn't think he was scheduled to work today, but this was the only place she could think to look for him.

She gave up on parking close to the Nature

Center and drove through the main lodge lot and around the rear of the building. Even the employee parking area looked full. Finally, a car pulled out and she slipped into a spot near the back entrance to the lodge offices.

Intent on finding Wes and letting him know how she felt about his vanishing act, she climbed out of her car and slammed the door. Before she'd taken three steps, she realized she'd forgotten her gloves and purse. Grumbling to herself, she pulled her keys from her pocket and walked back to unlock the car. She snatched her gloves and purse from the back seat and quickly locked the doors again.

"Hey, Lauren. Decide to come skiing after all?" Ryan's cheerful tone grated on her nerves.

She gritted her teeth and slowly turned to face him. "No, not today."

He smiled and stuffed his hands in his jacket pockets. "Come on. The snow's perfect. Let's have some fun."

She shook her head, her stomach tightening. She didn't have the patience or energy to deal with Ryan right now—not on top of everything else. Turning away, she headed toward the Nature Center.

"He's not there," Ryan called.

She spun around.

"You're looking for Wes, aren't you?"

She frowned, irritated he could so easily guess her plans.

His smile faded into a serious expression. "He doesn't work here anymore. I had to let him go."

She gasped. "You fired him?"

"I didn't have a choice. He wasn't honest with us about his past." He looked at the ground and shook his head. "I can't have someone like that working here, especially not with kids."

Fear crept up her spine. "What are you talking about?"

Ryan pressed his lips together, hesitating. "I'm sorry, Lauren. I hate to be the one to tell you this, but you'd find out sooner or later." He took a step closer and lowered his voice. "Wes was just released from prison last August."

She recoiled. "That's not true. Wes isn't a criminal."

"Tell that to the judge who put him there."

Shaking her head, she backed away. "Why would you lie to me about this?"

"I'm not lying, Lauren. He spent almost two years in prison."

"I don't believe you. He would've told me."

"He thought he could hide it from you and everyone else. When I confronted him, he gave me all kinds of excuses for not telling the truth." Ryan crossed his arms, looking disgusted. "He quit rather than be fired. He picked up his check earlier and said he's leaving town."

Her legs trembled as she turned and ran from Ryan. That was the most outrageous set of lies she'd ever heard. Wes couldn't be a convict!

But doubts rose and clouded her thoughts. He'd owned nothing except a backpack when they'd met, and he'd never explained his lack of roots. He always seemed to sidestep her questions about his past or give her vague answers. As their friendship grew, she'd accepted Wes's secrecy, but she'd never been totally comfortable with it. Were those uneasy feelings God's way of warning her to be careful of Wes? He said he'd had a rough time the past few years…but prison?

The incident with the photographer at Bower's Creek rose and filled her mind. Wes's anger and fear of being photographed made sense if he was trying to hide his identity or a disgraceful past.

Even if that was true, he'd never leave Tipton without saying goodbye to her and Toby, would he? Her stomach hit bottom.

She dashed up the Nature Center's steps and pulled on the door but discovered it was locked. She knocked and peered through the glass. Someone had to be there. She lifted her hand to continue her frantic knocking, but she stopped when she saw a hand-written sign tacked up on the bulletin board beside the door.

The Nature Center is closed Saturday morning March 10 due to an unexpected staff shortage. The winter bird trek is still on. We will leave at 8:30 a.m. and return at noon. The Nature Center will be open this afternoon after I return from the bird trek.

Thanks,

Bill Morgan, Head Naturalist, Wild River Nature Center

Lauren scanned the sign again and stared at the

words *unexpected staff shortage.* A shaft of pain pierced her heart. Hot tears burned her eyes.

Oh, Wes, why didn't you at least have the courage to tell me yourself?

Lauren pushed open the back door at Long Meadow and stepped inside. Her shoulders sagged and her heart felt like a heavy stone in her chest. How could she have been such a fool? Was she just naive where men were concerned, or did she wear a big sign around her neck that said, Wanted: Deceptive Man to Break My Heart. Only Those Who Can Pretend to Be Spiritual, Loving, and Sincere Need Apply.

Why hadn't she listened to her nagging doubts and sent Wes packing? Maybe then she could have avoided some of this heartbreak. But she'd let him stay in her home and wheedle his way into Toby's affections. How would she ever explain this to her son? Scolding herself for her stupidity, she shrugged off her coat and hung it on a hook.

"Wes, is that you?" Toby ran into the mudroom, his eyes wide with hope. As soon as he saw Lauren, his smile faded and his lower lip trembled. "I thought you were Wes."

"Sorry, sweetie." She reached for his hand. "Come on. We need to have a talk." Lauren led him to the kitchen table. As Toby climbed into his chair, she sent off a hurried prayer asking for a way to break the news to her son.

"Where's Wes? Didn't you find him? I thought he was coming over."

"No, Wes won't be coming over today."

"But we're working on a project." Toby's voice rose to a whiny, frightened pitch. "He said we'd get the rest of the wood this weekend."

She laid her hand over his, anguish twisting through her. "Toby, I don't think Wes will be spending any more time with us. He's leaving Tipton."

Panic flashed in his eyes. He jumped down from the chair. "No! He can't leave."

The heartbroken look on her son's face made her tremble. "He lost his job at the Nature Center, and without that—"

"He can get another job! Or he could live here and work on the barn. But he can't leave! You have to stop him!" Tears overflowed in Toby's eyes and cascaded down his cheeks. He turned and looked at Tilley as she walked into the kitchen.

Lauren sent her aunt a pleading look and then focused on her son. "I know you love Wes and you want him to stay, but sometimes things happen that are hard for little boys to understand."

His face turned stormy red. "I'm not a little boy! I'm bigger than you think!" He shoved over the closest chair, sending it crashing to the floor, and ran out of the kitchen.

"Toby, come back!" Lauren stood to go after him.

Tilley held out her hand to stop her. "Better let him settle down for a few minutes before you try to talk to him." Concern deepened the lines on her aunt's face as she crossed the kitchen. "What happened?"

"Wes is leaving." Lauren couldn't hold back her tears any longer.

Tilley touched Lauren's shoulder. "Oh, dear, I'm so sorry. Did you two have an argument?"

"No, he hasn't even talked to me." Lauren swiped at her tears and sniffed loudly. "I had to hear the truth from Ryan Zeller."

"What do you mean?"

"Wes has been in prison!" Lauren got up and snatched a tissue from the box on the counter.

Tilley sent her a serious, searching look. "I know, but I don't see—"

"You knew?"

"Yes, I recognized his name the first night he arrived, but I wasn't sure until he told me a little more about himself a few days later."

"Tilley! Why didn't you say something?"

Her aunt sighed. "I'm sorry, I thought it would be better for Wes to explain everything when he was ready."

"Well, he never did! He let me believe he was good and kind and trustworthy. He convinced me to let him spend time with Toby, and he made me fall in love with him." She sank down in her chair, laid her head down on her arm and sobbed.

"Lauren, don't you think you're overreacting just a little?"

She swiftly lifted her head. "No! He lied to me. And now he's lost his job and he's leaving town and he doesn't even have the nerve to tell me the truth."

"Just because he didn't explain everything doesn't mean he lied to you." Tilley leaned toward Lauren.

"You can understand why it's hard for him to talk about his time in prison. They were very cruel to him."

Lauren stared at her aunt. "What do you mean?"

Tilley frowned. "I thought you said you knew the truth."

"I thought I did."

Tilley lifted her silver brows. "He was arrested for his missionary work in the Middle East. They kept him in a terrible prison for more than a year and a half, and they treated him so badly it's a wonder he didn't die."

"He told you that?"

"No, he only said he used to be a missionary and wanted to start a new life. When I realized who he was, I went to the library and looked up several articles to learn more about his imprisonment."

Lauren closed her eyes, reeling from Tilley's explanation. She'd been wrong about Wes. So wrong. He wasn't an ex-con on the run out to deceive her and break her heart; he was a wounded man, seeking to rebuild his life and overcome the painful memories of persecution.

Her eyes flew open. "Why would Ryan fire him for that? It doesn't make sense. All he wanted to do was help hurting people. Why didn't Wes just explain?"

"I'm not sure. Something doesn't sound right about the whole situation."

"Why didn't Wes tell me what was going on? Surely he wouldn't think I'd be upset with him for being arrested for his missionary work." Lauren jumped up and paced across the kitchen. "Maybe if I talk to Ryan and explain everything, Wes could get his job back."

"I suppose it's worth a try, but the Zellers aren't known for listening to anyone else's advice or opinions." Tilley tapped her chin. "Let me show you those articles I copied at the library. I think you need to read them."

Lauren followed Tilley to her bedroom. Her aunt retrieved a file from her desk and together they sat on the bed and read the stories of Wes's imprisonment, trial and release. Tears flowed down Lauren's cheeks when she read about the beatings Wes endured and the death threats he lived with daily. How could she have ever doubted him? A deeper love and appreciation for him flooded her heart.

"It's a miracle he made it through and was finally released." Lauren tucked the articles back in the file.

"Yes, it truly is a miracle. People all over the world prayed for Wes. Our church's missions committee prayed for him every time we met. That's why I recognized his name the first night you brought him home."

Lauren blinked back tears and smiled at her aunt. "That's so awesome. And then he stayed with us and became our friend."

Tilley's eyes glowed. "That is a special reward, isn't it?"

"Yes, very special." Lauren stood, her hope renewed.

"I'm going to find him and straighten this out.

There's no reason for him to leave. If he doesn't get his job back at Wild River, he can work for me when I open the gallery." She wiped the last of the tears from her cheeks.

Tilley smiled. "Sounds like a fine idea."

"Pray for us, Tilley." Lauren hurried down the hall and into the kitchen. As she rushed past the table, a piece of notebook paper flew off and floated to the floor. The scrawl of childish writing caught her eye and she turned to pick it up. Large, determined letters filled the page.

> I am go in to stop Wes. Toby

Lauren stared at the message. Her hands began to shake. Fear squeezed the air from her lungs. She gasped for breath. "Tilley, come quick!"

"What is it, dear?" Tilley hobbled into the kitchen, her eyes wide.

"Look at this." Lauren held out the note to her aunt. "Does he think he can walk all the way to Wild River? I've got to find him!"

She stuffed the note in her pocket and ran to the mudroom. Toby's navy coat was missing, as well as his red hat and gloves.

Lauren grabbed her coat and yanked open the door. "Toby!" She frantically scanned the yard and path. Buttoning her coat against the chill, she hurried down the steps and followed the small set of footprints that left the driveway and disappeared into the trees beyond the woodshed.

Chapter Twenty-Four

Lauren trudged along the roadside, scanning the snow for her son's footprints. She hadn't seen a sign of his trail since it veered off their property and onto the road leading to Wild River. Tucking her freezing hands in her pockets, she picked up her pace.

She shouted her son's name and listened to her voice fade into the silent, snow-covered forest on both sides of the road. A frightening shiver raced down her arms. Where could he be? Why hadn't she overtaken him by now? Maybe she should go back for her car, but then how would she see his footprints? Her thoughts spun in crazy circles.

Oh, Lord, please help me find him.

She looked up as the sheriff's car sped around the bend and pulled to a stop next to her.

Sheriff Bob Bradley rolled down the window and looked out. "We got a call from your aunt. Any sign of Toby?" His serious expression made her believe he truly cared.

Lauren leaned toward his open window. "No, not yet."

Sheriff Bradley nodded. "Hop in and let me give you a ride home."

"But I've got to find my son. He's only six. He can't be out here by himself." Lauren's voice wobbled, and her gaze darted to the deserted road. How could she go home when her son was out here in the cold somewhere?

"Now, don't you worry. We'll find him. I've got a call out for the search-and-rescue team. They're meeting us at your house. The best thing you can do for Toby is come along with me. He'll want to see you as soon as we find him and bring him home."

Lauren swallowed, fighting her runaway emotions. Sheriff Bradley was right. Wandering down this road wasn't getting her any closer to finding Toby. She needed to turn the search over to trained people. Sheriff Bradley attended Tipton Community Church and was a good friend of Tilley's. She knew she could trust him.

Lauren climbed into his car. He asked her several questions about Toby as he drove. She answered each one and then showed him the note her son had left.

Five minutes later they pulled into the drive at Long Meadow. Three cars she didn't recognize were parked by the side of the house. One pulled a trailer containing two snowmobiles. A group of five men stood on the back porch talking to Tilley. Lauren climbed out of the sheriff's car and walked toward the house.

With tears in her eyes, Tilley hobbled down the

steps and hugged Lauren. "These are good men. They'll find him," she whispered.

Lauren closed her eyes and held on tight for several seconds. Finally, she released her aunt and they climbed the porch steps together.

Though her feet were numb from the cold, she didn't follow her aunt inside. Instead, she leaned against the porch railing and stared at the men gathered around the sheriff's car discussing plans for the search. Soon maps were spread out on the hood, and the sheriff began assigning search sectors to the men. But that did little to calm the churning in her stomach. Where was her son?

Bill's truck careened around the corner and raced up the drive. Two men rode in the cab.

Lauren grabbed the porch railing and held her breath. Before the truck rolled to a stop, Wes jumped from the passenger door and ran toward the house, bypassing the sheriff and his team.

He leaped up the porch steps. "We heard Toby was missing. What happened?" His eyes searched hers, reaching out with fearful, unspoken questions.

"He left this note." Lauren pulled the folded paper from her pocket and passed it to him with trembling hands.

Wes's dark brows knit together as he quickly scanned the words. He looked up at her and his eyes filled with painful understanding. "He wanted to stop me from leaving?"

Lauren pressed her lips together and nodded, her throat thick with emotion.

"How did he know?"

"I went to the Nature Center this morning looking for you. I ran into Ryan. He told me you quit and were leaving town."

Anger flashed in Wes's eyes when she mentioned Ryan's name.

"When I came home, Toby wanted to know why you didn't come over last night or today, so I told him you were leaving Tipton." Her voice fell to a choked whisper. "I was just trying to help him understand. I didn't know he would react like this."

Wes raked his hand through his hair, remorse etched on his face. "I'm sorry. I never wanted to hurt you or Toby." He closed his eyes and lowered his chin, the struggle evident on his face.

"I know," she said softly and laid her hand on his arm.

He looked up, his eyes edged with tears. "Forgive me, Lauren."

She nodded and blinked hard, trying to clear her own misty vision.

Bill hustled over to the bottom of the porch steps. "We're ready to go."

Wes glanced over his shoulder. "Okay, just a minute." He studied the note once more. Then he looked into Lauren's eyes with quiet determination. "We'll find him."

Her heart swelled. She reached for Wes and he wrapped his arms around her in a powerful embrace. Strength and confidence flowed through her as he held her close. For the first time since Toby had disappeared, a tiny flame of hope glowed in her heart.

She pulled back, sliding her hands down his coat

sleeves. He took one final moment to look into her eyes, then turned and strode down the steps to join Bill and the rest of the search team.

Wes stared out the truck window at the frozen forest. He and Bill had covered the first sector the sheriff had assigned them to without finding any sign of Toby's trail. Now they headed down Kaufman Road toward Wild River to search their next sector.

He squinted until the snowy trees became a silver blur, and his mind flashed back to his last glimpse of Lauren. She stood on the porch, watching them drive away, hope and trust shining in her eyes. He had to find Toby. There was no other option. He was responsible for his disappearance, and he wouldn't give up until he brought the boy home to Lauren.

He checked his watch and his stomach clenched. Toby had been out in the elements for almost four hours. He had to be cold by now and possibly dealing with the first stage of hypothermia.

Wes shifted in the seat and turned to Bill. "Can't you drive any faster?"

Bill sent him a worried glance. "We'll be there soon."

"I know, but it's getting late. We have to find him before dark." Wes rubbed his forehead. The message Toby had scribbled on his note burned in his memory.

Lord, show me where he is. Help me think like Toby.

He closed his eyes, remembering the times he had

spent with the boy and the adventures they'd shared. Suddenly, insight bolted through him. "Turn around!"

"What?" Bill darted a quick glance at him.

"Go back to town."

"Why? That's the opposite direction from Wild River."

"Toby doesn't know anything about directions. He's six. He goes by what he sees, not road signs or the points on a compass."

"Okay." Bill made a quick U-turn. "Where are we going?"

"Tipton Elementary. I took Toby sledding on that huge hill behind the school. There's a great view of Wild River from there. I pointed out the Nature Center and our house. He was really excited about it. Maybe he's trying to cross the valley and get to Wild River that way."

Bill shook his head. "There's nothing out there but thick wilderness. We better call the sheriff and get some more guys to meet us at the school."

Wes frowned and rubbed his chin. What if he was wrong and he pulled other searchers toward a dead end? "Let's check it out first and see if we find a trail. That shouldn't take long. We can call the sheriff if we come up with something."

Minutes later they pulled into the school parking lot and climbed out of the truck. Wes grabbed a backpack of emergency supplies and lifted it onto his shoulders. Bill did the same and they set out through the playground. Wes's boots crunched through the snow as they climbed the hill. Five boys and one little girl chased each other across the hillside and flew down the sledding path on inner tubes.

Bill headed toward the kids. "I'll find out if they've seen anyone dressed like Toby."

"I'll check up top." Wes continued his climb, scanning the snow for footprints leading away from the sledding path. Several distinct prints criss-crossed the hillside, but as he crested the hill most of them disappeared. He lifted his gaze toward Wild River on the other side of the deep valley. Wes estimated it was at least three miles, maybe four. If his guess was correct, Toby's trail should lead east from here, downhill into the forest.

"Wes!" Bill charged up the hill, his expression jubilant. "They saw him!" Panting, he met Wes at the top. "The little girl is in Toby's class. She saw him a while ago and asked him to go sledding with them. He turned her down."

Wes's hopes soared. "She's sure it was Toby?"

"She sounded pretty certain."

"Did she see where he went?"

Bill shook his head. "That's all she could tell me."

Wes and Bill scanned the hilltop and discovered two sets of footprints leading away from the sledding area. Both looked to be about Toby's size. They decided to split up and each follow one trail, checking back with each other by radio every ten minutes. As Wes started his descent into the quiet forest, he heard Bill call the sheriff and tell him they were searching in a new area.

Now that Wes had a firm lead and a trail to follow, adrenaline pumped through his system, giving him a new spurt of energy. Toby couldn't be too far off. He stopped and called his name, then strained to listen. A bright red cardinal flew from a tree branch overhead and sent a small shower of feathery flakes down on Wes. Nothing else stirred.

Wes shrugged his shoulders, moving the pack to a more comfortable position, and focused on the trail of footprints. His face tingled from the cold, but he pressed on. About ten minutes later his radio beeped. He pulled it from his backpack and listened to Bill's update.

"My trail turned south, crossed a fence and led to the backyard of a home on one of Tipton's side streets. The little boy living there confirmed seeing Toby at the sledding hill, but he didn't have any other helpful information."

"I must be on the right track."

"Yep. I'm heading back to the school." Bill's voice crackled over the radio. "I'll call you when I get there."

"Okay. Stay in touch." Wes whispered a prayer of thanks and clipped the radio to his belt. He set off again, hope making his steps lighter.

When he reached the bottom of the valley, he found a small creek. Icy crystals clung to the rocks at the side, making the going slippery. Sloshing through water that almost reached the top of his boots, he crossed the stream and reached the other side.

He slowed and scanned the snow, searching for

Toby's tracks. Only a few tiny animal prints led to and from the stream. A cold knot formed in his stomach. He couldn't lose the trail. Not now. Not when he was so close.

He scanned the woods, calling Toby's name for the hundredth time. Only the silence answered.

Heading downstream, he searched the icy bank and finally spotted the trail. Frowning, Wes kneeled in the snow. Toby's footprints were closer together now, with sliding scuff marks instead of the clear, strong impressions he'd seen earlier. The boy was getting tired, dragging his feet. That slower pace would make it easier for Wes to catch up, but it also meant Toby's physical condition was worsening.

Wes ducked under a low hanging branch, scanning the area. A flash of navy-blue up ahead caught his eye. His heart raced. "Toby!" His shout echoed off the silent trees.

Wes broke into a run, dodging branches and scrambling over rocks. The blue lump lying on the frozen ground didn't move.

Lauren paced to the front window and pushed the curtain aside. Anxiety wrapped around her chest like a tight band, cutting off her ability to take a deep breath. Why hadn't they found Toby yet? Surely with ten trained men searching they could find one little boy.

Staring out the window, she shivered and rubbed her arms. The sheriff had gone outside to greet three more searchers who had just arrived in a dark green SUV with Wild River Ski Resort emblazoned on the door. They were probably men from the resort's ski patrol here to join the search. The sheriff had told her they were on their way.

He spread his map out on the hood of their SUV and the men gathered around. One man leaned over the map and asked him a question, but the sheriff held up his hand and pulled a shortwave radio from his belt.

Lauren tensed as she watched his serious expression change. He swung around and faced the men, motioning them closer. Jabbing his finger at the map, he smiled and slapped the nearest man on the back.

Lauren's heart leaped. She ran for the door and jerked it open. "Did you hear something?"

Sheriff Bradley jogged toward her, a hopeful look on his face. "A little girl sledding behind the elementary school reported seeing Toby there. Bill Morgan and Wes Evans are following two trails from the sledding area now."

A tidal wave of relief washed over her. "Do you think it's Toby's trail?"

"We don't have any other leads, so I'm going to call in some of the other searchers and head over there. I'll call an ambulance to meet us at the school parking lot, just in case we need it. You want to ride over with me?"

"You go ahead. I have to tell Tilley. I'll come in my car as soon as I get my coat." She ran back into the house and relayed the news to her aunt, who gave a happy shout. Then Lauren rushed toward the mudroom to get her coat, hat and gloves.

Tilley followed. "I'll stay here and get dinner going. Let me know the minute they find him. And invite Wes and all those nice men back here. They deserve a hot meal after all they're doing to find our Toby." Her aunt lifted her eyes toward Heaven. "Oh, Father, thank You for this encouraging news. Be with those searchers. Guide their every step. Help them find Toby soon!"

"Amen!" Lauren gave her aunt a quick hug and flew out the door.

Chapter Twenty-Five

The orange sun hung low in the western sky, casting long purple shadows across the snowy playground. Lauren blew on her glove-covered hands and scanned the empty hillside beyond the school property.

The sheriff had sent two other searchers down to help Wes and Bill follow the trail they hoped would lead to Toby. Her stomach tensed as she peered at the sinking sun. The temperature had already dropped several degrees and soon darkness would make their search more difficult.

Remembering the scarf she'd left in the back seat of her car, she walked away from the sheriff and crossed the parking lot.

Everything is going to be okay, she told herself. She had to believe that. Closing her eyes, she slowed her steps and breathed a silent prayer. *Father, please bring Wes and Toby back safely. You know how much*

*I love them, how much I need them. There are so
many things I want to say. Please give me that
chance.*

She heard a car approach and opened her eyes.
A silver BMW raced into the school parking lot and
squealed to a stop. She squinted, trying to look
through the tinted side window to see who sat in the
driver's seat.

The door opened and Arthur Zeller stepped out.

Her stomach clenched. Seven years had greatly
changed his appearance. His thick, wavy hair had
vanished and only a silver fringe remained. His
shoulders drooped and deep anxiety lines etched
his once-handsome face.

He glanced at her with penetrating blue-gray eyes
so much like his sons' and Toby's. "We heard your
little boy is lost," he said, then bit his lip and seemed
to struggle to hold back his emotions.

Before she could answer, Ryan climbed out of
the passenger side and stood to face her, a cold,
haughty look on his face.

She clenched her fists inside her gloves and
glared at him. "What are you doing here?"

"We want to help find the boy," Mr. Zeller added
before his son could speak.

Lauren focused on Ryan. "You have a lot of
nerve showing up here. Toby never would've run
away if you hadn't told me that distorted story about
Wes. He was trying to stop him from leaving town."

Ryan sent his father a guilty glance and then
looked back at her. "Everything I said about Wes
Evans is true."

A hot surge of righteous anger flashed through her. "No! You twisted the truth into a lie. Wes isn't a criminal and you know it. He was sent to prison for his missionary work in the Middle East."

"Where did you hear a story like that? From Wes?"

"No, he's too humble to tell me about it. I read it on the Internet."

Ryan snorted. "You better check your facts. When I confronted him, he admitted he'd never told you the truth. How can you trust someone like that?"

"I don't need to know every detail about his past to trust him." The cold wind whipped a long strand of hair across her face. She swiped it away. "Since the first day Wes came to Tipton, he's proven himself to me over and over. You had no grounds to fire him."

"I didn't fire him. He quit."

Mr. Zeller scowled at his son. "Ryan, what have you done?" His voice sounded like the growl of an angry bear.

Ryan huffed. "You don't understand, Dad. It's complicated."

"Well, I know this much—If my grandson gets hurt as a result of your foolish shenanigans, you won't be taking over Wild River."

"Come on, Dad. She's blowing this out of proportion. It's not my fault. I can explain."

"Oh, you're right about that. You have a lot of explaining to do. But right now I want you to go talk to the sheriff about joining the search."

"But Dad, I don't—"

"Don't *but Dad* me! Get over there right now or you can head home and pack your bags."

Ryan flashed a heated glance at Lauren. Then he turned and stalked off toward the searchers gathered around the sheriff's car and ambulance.

Mr. Zeller rubbed his forehead. "I don't know all the details, but Ryan said your boy is Stephen's son. Is that right?"

She swallowed and nodded, but she lifted her chin and held his gaze.

Tears flooded the old man's eyes. "I'm sorry. I didn't know." He sniffed and looked off toward the mountains. "I loved my son, but he had a wild spirit I could never tame. He wasn't all bad. He had good qualities, too. I thought he'd turned a corner and was getting his life straightened out before the accident but…"

She nodded and pressed her lips together.

"Did he know about the boy?"

She shook her head, shame and fear waging a brief battle in her heart. But the truth she had learned about forgiveness softened the memories and caused her to see the pain in the old man's face. "I'm sorry you lost your son. You must have loved him very much."

Mr. Zeller nodded and blinked away his tears. "Yes…I did. You're a parent now, you know how much you love your children no matter what they do." His gaze moved to follow Ryan as he talked to the sheriff. "I'm sorry for the trouble Ryan caused. I don't understand it all, but I'll get to the bottom of it. He may be twenty-seven, but he still needs a lot of prayer and guidance. And I intend to see that he gets it."

Mr. Zeller's words sent a ripple of surprise through her. Had the tragedies in his family sparked a sincere faith in his heart? Perhaps her fears of him were based on old rumors and small-town gossip. Maybe Toby could have a relationship with his grandfather someday.

"Lauren!"

She spun at the sheriff's call.

He jogged toward her across the parking lot. "They found Toby! They're bringing him out now."

Relief weakened her knees. "Is he all right?"

"They say he's cold and tired but seems fine other than that."

Mr. Zeller grabbed the sheriff's arm. "Do you need any more men or equipment? You can use whatever we've got at Wild River."

"Thank you, sir, but we don't need anything else right now. I appreciate you sending over your ski patrol earlier. Those men have worked hard all afternoon."

"Did one of them find the boy?"

"No, sir, it was Wes Evans. I understand he works for you at the Nature Center."

Mr. Zeller nodded and smiled at Lauren. "Yes, he certainly does."

Wes's heartbeat pounded in his ears as he climbed the slippery hillside. Toby rode on his back with his little arms wrapped tightly around Wes's neck. Though the boy weighed no more than the pack Wes had carried around Europe, Wes's legs and chest burned from the brisk pace of their steep climb. But he had to keep pushing if he was going to get Toby out of the valley before nightfall.

Bill and the other two searchers hiked ahead of him. Bill glanced over his shoulder, concern creasing his forehead. "You want me to take a turn carrying him?"

"No. I'm okay." Wes didn't want to waste time shifting packs and transferring Toby. They had to be near the top. He looked up. Dusk cast deep shadows across their path. The sky glowed golden and crimson above the dark trees scattered over the hillside.

"Are we almost there?" Toby's voice sounded weaker, sending another shaft of worry through Wes. He didn't seem to be injured, but he was cold and exhausted from his long trek through the woods.

"Not much farther now. You just hang on."

Toby tightened his hold around Wes's neck. "You're not really leaving, are you?"

This was the third time he'd asked that question. Each time it cut a little deeper. Wes longed to say he'd never leave, but how could he make that promise? He hadn't kept his word to stay away from Lauren and leave Tipton. What would happen when he got back? Wes refused to worry about it. Returning Toby safely to Lauren was all that mattered. Even though he had radioed ahead, he knew she would still be worried until she held her son in her arms.

"Let's just focus on getting home and seeing your mom."

"Okay." Toby laid his head on Wes's shoulder and snuggled closer. "I'm glad you found me. I love you, Wes."

Wes's chest tightened. "I love you, too, buddy."

Climbing over a large downed tree, he followed Bill's path. They pushed through a tangled clump of underbrush and crested the hilltop. New energy surged through Wes. They were almost home.

He smiled and pointed to the playground. "Look, there's your school. And see those people in the parking lot?" The boy nodded. "I bet your mom's down there with the sheriff and all the guys who've been looking for you."

"Mom!" Toby strained forward and waved, though Wes felt certain he couldn't see Lauren yet.

"This ought to get their attention." Bill raised his fingers to his mouth, blew an ear-piercing whistle and waved both arms overhead.

"Hold on, Toby." Wes grabbed the boy's legs more tightly and jogged toward the group gathered at the edge of the parking lot.

Toby giggled and held on for dear life. In their rush, they almost tumbled down the sledding hill, but Wes regained his balance and hurried on. In less than a minute, Wes crossed the snowy playground and strode into the parking lot to the cheers of the sheriff and searchers, Bill and the other two searchers close behind. The waiting men rushed forward, shouting happy greetings and slapping Wes on the back.

As Wes swung Toby around and lowered him to the ground, pain shot up his back like an electric shock. He gritted his teeth and pulled in a sharp breath.

One of the EMTs stepped forward. "How are you doing, Toby?" The young man knelt beside the boy and began asking him questions and checking him over.

Wes hobbled a couple steps, trying to figure out what he'd done to his back. Was it just muscle strain or had he done some serious damage? He took a couple more tentative steps to see if he could just walk off the pain.

The sheriff clamped a strong hand on Wes's shoulder.

Wes grimaced and fought off the stinging twinge shooting down his spine.

"Good work, Wes. Your idea to search that valley probably saved that little boy's life."

The sheriff's words barely registered as Wes scanned the crowd, searching for Lauren. Surely she would've heard Bill's whistle or the searchers' cheers. He turned to the sheriff. "Where's Lauren?"

A puzzled look settled on Sheriff Bradley's face. "I just spoke to her a few minutes ago."

One of the searchers in a red ski jacket with Wild River Ski Resort stitched on the front touched his arm. "I saw her talking to Art and Ryan Zeller over there." He pointed across the parking lot.

Alarm surged through Wes. What was Ryan doing here? Then he saw Lauren emerge from behind a large van and run toward them, tears streaking her face.

"Toby!" She pushed through the crowd and reached for her son. Dropping to her knees, she pulled him into her tight embrace.

"Mom." He melted against her, his chin trembling and tears trickling down his cheeks.

Wes stood by, watching their reunion with a lump as huge as a boulder clogging his throat. He didn't care what he'd done to his back. This was worth it.

Lauren finally released Toby and leaned back to look him over. "Are you okay, honey?"

Toby nodded and sniffed. "Yeah, I'm fine."

"I was so worried about you." She brushed his hair back off his forehead, searching his face.

"I'm sorry. I was looking for Wes, but he found me." Toby smiled up at Wes with shining eyes.

Lauren's expression reflected the same tender emotions as she shifted her gaze to Wes.

He limped toward Lauren, and after three steps held her in his arms.

A shadow of concern touched her face. "You're limping. What happened?"

"Don't worry. It's nothing. Toby's safe. That's all that matters."

She laid her head on his chest and hung on tight, like she never wanted to let go. "Thank you for finding him. That means the world to me."

Emotion tightened his throat, stealing away the words he longed to say. Closing his eyes, he pulled her closer and kissed the top of her head.

He couldn't leave her—not now, not ever. A prayer rose from his heart. *Oh, Father, please protect us and make a way for us to always be together.*

Chapter Twenty-Six

Lauren grimaced as she watched Wes haul himself up from the couch and slowly walk Bill to the front door at Long Meadow. He slowed and leaned against the wall, his face lined with weariness.

She followed, wishing she could convince him to obey the doctor's orders and stay off his feet tonight. Memories of her ride in the ambulance with Toby and Wes flashed through her mind. She'd focused on comforting her son, but she'd been concerned for Wes, too. Though his back injury didn't look serious, they'd taken X-rays at the hospital and finally sent him home with painkillers and orders to take it easy for a few days.

Rather than lying down, Wes had insisted on eating dinner with the rest of the searchers when they'd returned to Long Meadow. He would've helped with the dishes if Tilley hadn't shooed him out of the kitchen. Then he'd taken up residence on the couch in the living room, exchanging stories with Bill and a few of the other men who had stayed for dessert and coffee. Toby hovered near them all evening, unwilling to let her or Wes out of his sight until Lauren finally carried her exhausted son to bed.

Bill grabbed his coat from the back of the chair and tugged it on. "This has sure been a wild day. Glad Toby's home safe and you're okay."

"Thanks, Bill." Wes exchanged a meaningful look with his friend.

Bill gave Wes a cautious hug. He stepped back and smiled. "You sure you don't want me to hang around and be your chauffeur? I could read the paper in the kitchen and help Tilley clean up if you two want to talk."

"No, you can head home. We'll work something out." Wes glanced at Lauren with a loving look that sent a clear message. He wanted time alone with her.

She smiled and returned the same message with her eyes. "I can drive you home later."

"Nonsense! Wes is staying here tonight." Tilley bustled through the living room carrying an empty tray. "We need to keep an eye on that back injury. No need to jostle him around by driving him home tonight. The guest room is all made up."

Bill grinned. "Okay. I guess I'll see you tomorrow, then." He lifted his hand to wave and walked out the door.

Tilley set her tray on the coffee table and began clearing the dessert plates and empty cups. "I'll just

load these in the dishwasher and then head to bed."
She looked up at Lauren. "Why don't you two sit
down and enjoy the fire?"

Lauren smiled. "Thanks, Tilley."

Humming a little tune, her aunt carried the tray
through the kitchen door and closed it behind her.

Wes took Lauren's hand and led her to the couch.
"Sit with me."

"Are you sure you're not too tired? The doctor
said you should rest."

"I'm fine. I just need some time with you." He
tossed aside a pillow and sat down. She settled on
the couch next to him. He put his arm around her
and pulled her closer.

She leaned her head on his shoulder and sighed
softly. The fire crackled and sent the faint smell of
wood smoke into the room. A bayberry candle
burned on the mantel, adding its comforting scent.
If only she could hold on to this peaceful feeling…but some secrets still separated them.

"Were you really leaving town?" she asked.

"Yes." His somber tone sent a shiver through
her.

"Why? I don't understand." She lifted her head
and looked at him. "Is it because of what happened
in the Middle East?"

Surprise and then regret flashed in his eyes. "I'm
sorry, Lauren. So many times I wanted to explain."
He stared into the fire. The muscles in his jaw flickered.

"It's all right. I know all about it," she said softly.
"I read the articles."

His gaze shifted back to her. "What articles?"

"Tilley thought she recognized your name the first night she met you. She went to the library and copied some magazine articles off the Internet, but she didn't show them to me until this morning. She wanted to give you time to explain things."

He nodded, sadness shadowing his dark eyes. "I should've told you about it a long time ago. But that's not why I was leaving." He fixed his serious gaze on her. "Yesterday, Ryan called me down to the office and quizzed me about my past. When he realized he couldn't scare me off by threatening to tell everyone about it, he said he'd go to court and take Toby away from you if I didn't leave town and promise to never contact you again."

"What?! That's crazy. How did he think he was going to get away with it?"

"He said he had enough money to hire a high-powered lawyer and prove you weren't a good mother. He took pictures of you and Toby that looked incriminating. He was the photographer who followed us at Bower's Creek."

She huffed out a disgusted breath. "Well, that might have been his plan. But I don't think we have to worry about it now. When Toby disappeared, his father got wind of it and began asking questions. Ryan told him part of the story and they showed up at the school to help with the search."

"Did you talk to them?"

She nodded. "I told Mr. Zeller how Ryan had lied to me about your past and how that made Toby run away. He was so mad he told Ryan that if anything happened to Toby he could forget about inheriting Wild River." The memory of Mr. Zeller's tears filled her thoughts. "He got very emotional when he learned he had a grandson."

"You told him Stephen was Toby's father?"

"No, Ryan did. I think he wanted to use it against us. But it backfired and brought Mr. Zeller around to our side. He said he was sorry for the trouble Ryan caused and promised to get to the bottom of it. He also said you still have a job at the Nature Center if you want it."

Wes smiled. "I suppose if Mr. Zeller can keep Ryan in line I'd consider it."

"I'm sorry I believed what Ryan said about you. I should've known it wasn't true, but I couldn't find you, and I was so confused." Tears clouded her vision as she recalled the pain of the morning and the frantic search for her son. She closed her eyes and laid her head on his shoulder again.

Wes released a heavy sigh. "I'm sorry, Lauren. If I'd told you the truth about my past, Ryan would never have had so much power over us. I want to tell you what really happened."

His words infused her with hope. She lifted her head and looked into his eyes. "I'd like that."

"I was a missionary in the Middle East for six years," he said slowly, taking her hand.

Over the next half hour, Wes opened his heart and told her about his arrest and imprisonment. As she listened, she learned much more than she'd read in the magazine articles—details of God's grace and provision even in the darkest prison. She fought tears many times as he described the interrogations and beatings.

"I couldn't convince them I was telling the truth, and they wouldn't give up the crazy idea that I worked for the CIA. They told me I'd be executed if I didn't confess. But how could I confess to something that wasn't true?

"One day, they brought out pictures of my co-workers and friends. They demanded I write down their names and tell them exactly what my relationship was to each one of them. At first I refused, but the beatings got so bad I finally broke down and told them the truth about our work.

"After that, the interrogations became less frequent. In a few weeks, I was released, but at what cost—the lives of my friends?"

Releasing her hand, he bowed his head and pinched the top of his nose. "I caved in to save my own skin." The despair in his voice pierced her heart.

"No, Wes. That's not true. You told the truth to evil people, and they used it for evil purposes. That's not your fault."

"I should've been willing to lay down my life to protect my friends. But I couldn't do it. I'll never forgive myself for that." He closed his eyes, his fight against powerful emotions evident on his face.

She took his hand again. "You don't have to forgive yourself, Wes. Jesus forgives you."

He shook his head, avoiding her gaze.

"Hey, aren't you the one who showed me those

great verses about God's forgiveness? You said our sins are removed…as far as the east is from the west, remember?"

Pain still clouded his eyes as he looked at her. "Your situation was different. You weren't a Christian when you were involved with Stephen. I've been a believer for years and a missionary on top of that. I should've been able to trust God and make it through my time in prison without compromising the lives of the people I loved."

Tears glistened in his eyes. "Don't you understand? I'm not fit to be a missionary, and I don't think I'd make a very good husband and father for you and Toby. You need someone strong and committed, someone you can count on to be there and see you through, not some guy who's going to bail on you the first time things get difficult."

She stared at him, stunned by his words. "Wes, you're so wrong. Look at what happened today. You could've told the sheriff where you thought Toby was and sent someone else to search for him, but you went yourself and you brought him back to me." She touched his cheek. "You're a man with deep convictions and amazing strength. You've proven that over and over since the first day you arrived."

His dark gaze met hers, a hint of hope glowing there.

"God's not looking for perfection, Wes. He's looking for perseverance."

She got up and crossed the room to retrieve her Bible from the desk in the corner. "I found this verse the other day." She thumbed through the pages as she walked back to the couch. "Here it is." She sat down beside him again. "If we claim to be without sin, we deceive ourselves and the truth is not in us. If we confess our sins, He is faithful and just and will forgive us our sins and purify us from all un-righteousness."

She looked up at him. "God knows we're going to fall and fail sometimes. That's why we need a savior and a way to handle the sin we all struggle against every day. He wants us to know we can live a life of freedom and forgiveness."

Wes sighed and stared into the fire again. "For so long, I've avoided even praying about this. Just asking God for forgiveness seemed too easy when what I did risked the lives of so many people."

"Forgiveness is a priceless gift," she said softly. "There's nothing easy about it. It cost God a tremendous amount to send His Son to pay for our sins. But He did it because He loves us and wants a close relationship with us, free of guilt and regrets."

"I know what you're saying is true, but believing it and accepting God's forgiveness won't change what happened to my friends. Some of them were arrested, and others may have been killed because of their friendship with me and their belief in the Gospel. Every day I wonder what's happened to them."

A smile tugged at her lips, but she held it back. "I think I know."

Surprise flashed across his face. "How could you?"

"There was a follow-up article published about two months ago. Tilley showed it to me this morning with the others. It said all your coworkers from World Outreach have been released and safely reassigned to other countries. And the local people who were arrested have all been set free, except for one man they called R.H. His letters have been smuggled out of prison and sent to his hometown. They say some of his family and friends have become believers because of his powerful testimony from prison."

A faint smile lifted his lips. "That's got to be my friend Raheem. He's an amazing guy with awesome faith. He wants to be a pastor."

"It looks like he already is." She laid her hand on his arm. "Don't you see, Wes, that what those prison officials meant for evil, God turned around for good? Your imprisonment and even your confession have all been redeemed and turned into something God can use. His plan is bigger than we can imagine, and His power is stronger than any earthly government. Don't limit Him or refuse His love and forgiveness."

Wes blinked the moisture away from his eyes. "You are a very wise woman."

"Please stay in Tipton," she said softly. "I couldn't bear it if you went away."

He stroked her cheek. "I'd be a fool to leave you and Toby. You're the family I've always dreamed of. I love you, Lauren," he whispered, his voice thick.

His sweet words melted her heart, and all her doubts and questions vanished. "I love you, too. I never expected to find someone so special. Then you came into my life—and along came love."

He studied her a long moment, his expression full of tenderness. Then he cupped her face in his hand and kissed her.

She returned his kiss, lingering, savoring the sweetness of the moment. Wes loved her. He wasn't leaving. They had time for their love to grow and enjoy all the Lord had planned for them.

The fire crackled and hissed, and the steady drip of melting snow serenaded them with a plip-plop sound as it fell from the gutter and landed on the porch.

Wes sighed and leaned his head back against the couch. "Hear that?"

She snuggled closer, contentment flowing through her. "Yes. It must be warming up. Winter's almost over."

Wes chuckled. "Well, there are still two more weeks until it's officially spring."

"Good thing. I'll need every minute to finish setting up the gallery."

He twirled a strand of her hair around his finger. "Sounds like you could use some more help."

"Know anyone who might be available?"

"Hmm. Maybe."

"Well, the pay may not be too great, but the benefit package will make it worthwhile," she added with a teasing smile.

Grinning, he lifted his brows. Then he leaned down and kissed her again, promising a love that would carry them into a future filled with new hopes and dreams.

Dear Reader,

Thanks for reading my first Love Inspired novel, *Along Came Love*. Lauren and Wes became a very important part of my life as I wrote their story. Lauren's love for her family, her desire to open her own gallery and her longing to find lasting love made her dear to my heart. Wes's quiet kindness and deep faith made him a very special hero.

Their struggle to understand and accept God's forgiveness and love is an important journey we all need to take. Many people know that God forgives, yet they have a hard time trusting God and believing what He says in His Word about this important topic. I hope the lessons Wes and Lauren learned will speak to your heart. Please remember God's arms are always open. He is waiting for you to come to Him, pour out your sorrows and failures and receive His complete forgiveness. Jesus makes all this possible for us. What a wonderful Savior!

I'd love to hear from you. You may e-mail me at carrie@carrieturansky.com or visit my Web site www.carrieturansky.com.

Carrie Turansky

QUESTIONS FOR DISCUSSION

1. When Lauren met Wes she made several assumptions about him because of his appearance. What made her change her mind? How important is outward appearance? Do you usually look past the surface, or are you quick to make a judgment based on the way someone looks?

2. Wes wanted to hide his past from Lauren. Why do you think he felt that need? Have you ever tried to hide your failures or sins from God or others? Were you successful? How did that make you feel?

3. Wes felt he had failed God during his imprisonment. When he arrived in Vermont he wondered if God could still use him to help Lauren and Toby. Have you ever felt as if you failed a test God set before you? What insight does Psalm 51 give you about forgiveness, restoration and helping others?

4. Toby's lack of a father figure seemed to add to his struggles. What did Lauren do to help her son overcome this? How can single parents ensure that their children's emotional needs are met? What can you do to help single parents?

5. Though Lauren had become a Christian and asked for forgiveness, she still felt a sense of guilt and shame for her past sins and poor choices. Why did she continue to carry those burdens? How does relying on our emotions or feelings about our sins sometimes lead us astray? How does I John 1:9 give insight for her situation?

6. Toby's struggles in school put a lot of pressure on Lauren, but God used those problems to draw her and Wes closer. Have you ever looked back and seen God bring good out of difficult situations in your life?

7. Wes was willing to leave town to protect Lauren and Toby and to ensure they could remain together. What do you think of his choice? What does I Corinthians 13 say about love? Which of these characteristics do you see Wes showing in his decision to place Lauren and Toby's happiness above his own?